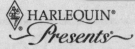

HARLEQUIN®
Presents

Harlequin Presents never fails to bring you the most gorgeous, brooding alpha heroes—so don't miss out on this month's irresistible collection!

THE ROYAL HOUSE OF NIROLI series continues with Susan Stephens's *Expecting His Royal Baby*. The king has found provocative prince Nico Fierezza a suitable bride. But Carrie has been in love with Nico—her boss— for years, and after one night of passion is pregnant!

When handsome Peter Ramsey discovers Erin's having his baby in *The Billionaire's Captive Bride* by Emma Darcy, he offers her the only thing he can think of to guarantee his child's security—marriage! In *The Greek Tycoon's Unwilling Wife* by Kate Walker, Andreas has lost his memory, but what will happen when he recalls throwing Rebecca out of his house on their wedding day—for reasons only he knows? If you're feeling festive, you'll love *The Boss's Christmas Baby* by Trish Morey, where a boss discovers his convenient mistress is expecting his baby. In *The Spanish Duke's Virgin Bride* by Chantelle Shaw, ruthless Spanish billionaire Duke Javier Herrera sees in Grace an opportunity for revenge *and* a contract wife! In *The Italian's Pregnant Mistress* by Cathy Williams, millionaire Angelo Falcone has Francesca in his power and in his bed, and this time he won't let her go. In *Contracted: A Wife for the Bedroom* by Carol Marinelli, Lily knows Hunter's ring will only be on her finger for twelve months, but soon a year doesn't seem long enough! Finally, brand-new author Susanne James brings you *Jed Hunter's Reluctant Bride*, where Jed demands Cryssie marry him because it makes good business sense, but Cryssie's feelings run deeper…. Enjoy!

IN Bed WITH THE Boss

Chosen by him for business,
taken by him for pleasure...

A classic collection of office romances from
Harlequin Presents, by your favorite authors.

Look out for more, coming soon!

Trish Morey

THE BOSS'S CHRISTMAS BABY

HARLEQUIN®

TORONTO • NEW YORK • LONDON
AMSTERDAM • PARIS • SYDNEY • HAMBURG
STOCKHOLM • ATHENS • TOKYO • MILAN • MADRID
PRAGUE • WARSAW • BUDAPEST • AUCKLAND

ISBN-13: 978-0-373-12678-1
ISBN-10:   0-373-12678-6

THE BOSS'S CHRISTMAS BABY

First North American Publication 2007.

Copyright © 2007 by Trish Morey.

www.eHarlequin.com

Printed in U.S.A.

All about the author…
Trish Morey

TRISH MOREY wrote her first book at age eleven for a children's book-week competition. Entitled *Island Dreamer,* it proved to be her first rejection. Shattered and broken, she turned to a life where she could combine her love of fiction with her need for creativity—and became a chartered accountant☺. Life wasn't all dull, though, as she embarked on a skydiving course, completing three jumps before deciding that she'd given her fear of heights a run for its money.

Meanwhile, she fell in love and married a handsome guy who cut computer code. After the birth of their second daughter, Trish spied an article saying that Harlequin was actively seeking new authors. It was one of those "Eureka!" moments—Trish was going to be one of those authors!

Eleven years after reading that fateful article, the magical phone call came and Trish finally realized her dream. According to Trish, writing and selling a book is a major life achievement that ranks right up there with jumping out of an airplane, and motherhood. All three take commitment, determination and sheer guts, but the effort is so very, very worthwhile.

Trish now lives with her husband and four young daughters in a special part of South Australia, surrounded by orchards and bushland and visited by the occasional koala and kangaroo.

You can visit Trish at her website at www.trishmorey.com or e-mail her at trish@trishmorey.com.

To Morgan and Tegan.
Two real-life heroines who have life, love and
adventures galore just waiting to happen.
Here's to finding your happily ever afters.

CHAPTER ONE

MAVERICK hated to be kept waiting. He prowled through the waiting room that separated his Gold Coast office from his PA's, only to find her computer monitor ominously dark and the flicker of numbers on the digital clock the only flash of movement, highlighting in brilliant red the full extent of his PA's transgressions. Nine-fifteen and still no sign of her!

Where was she? Still sulking after he'd refused her a week's leave? Or just taking it easy because she thought he was out of the country and he'd never know? Whatever; if this was the way she got it into her head to act when he wasn't around, then she was in for a *big* surprise. He didn't pay her the kind of megabucks he did so that she could sleep in whenever she thought she'd get away with it. She was a good operator, but nobody was *that* good.

With a growl he wheeled around and stormed back into his office, slamming the door in irritation. The noise reverberated around the room, echoing his mood. *Damn right,* he thought, throwing himself into his chair and tugging on his tie, his fury mounting by the second.

Now that the European end of the deal was on hold

indefinitely, it was more critical than ever that the Rogerson contract be shored up, and fast. It couldn't wait. *And neither could he!*

So where the hell was that woman?

What a morning! Over the music playing on her iPod, Tegan Fielding let fly an uncharacteristic string of curses aimed squarely at the universe in general, and her sister in particular, as the lift doors slid open, releasing her to the plush executive floor that would be her workaday home for the next week.

Without a break in her tirade, a sweep of her eyes took in her dimly lit surroundings—the skilfully screened open-plan office just beyond the lifts, with the rest of the entire floor devoted entirely to the boss's office suite beyond. Everything was just as Morgan had described. Without checking, she already knew that to the left behind the lift well would be the fully stocked kitchen and bar, and to the right the bathrooms. The public bathrooms, at least. There was another executive *en suite*, Morgan had told her, attached to Maverick's private rooms beyond his office that he used when he worked late. But that was academic. She didn't plan on stepping anywhere near that hallowed turf in the next few days if she could help it.

Still muttering, she slapped at a bank of light switches on the wall, slammed down her bag on the desk and pulled out a new packet of stockings. Morgan had warned her to be beware of the old lady with the broken gate and two over-enthusiastic bitser puppies who lived near the bus stop, but she hadn't been expecting to run into them quite so soon or with such devastating consequences. By the time they'd lost interest and found a new victim to harass, Tegan's stockings had been laddered beyond repair, and her navy skirt patterned in paw prints so badly that Mrs Garrett had insisted on sponging them off for her.

It would have been quicker to walk home and get changed. As it was, she'd seen two buses arrive and depart while the old woman had tried valiantly to work some kind of white-spirits magic on her skirt. An emergency stop at a pharmacist around the corner from the office had taken care of replacement stockings. And finally she was here.

So much for Morgan's paranoia that she would be late. Tegan gave an ironic laugh. 'A stickler for time,' Morgan had called her boss, a total despot when it came to extracting his money's worth from his employees. Well, Tegan had tried to get here on time and look what had happened. Besides, what did it matter anyway? He wasn't even here.

She pulled the lace-topped stockings from their packet and let their sheer silkiness slip over her hands. She'd been unable to find the same brand as the sensible support-stockings filling an entire drawer of her twin's walk-in wardrobe, and the only reason she'd agreed to pay the outrageous price they'd been asking for these was the knowledge that Morgan was paying all her expenses for the week and a sizeable bonus into the deal. Her sister's stockings were nice enough, but these were gossamer thin and silky sheer. After three years working in far-flung refugee camps, and no immediate job prospects on her return, if a decent pay cheque was a rare temptation, then the feel of silky stockings against her skin was downright decadence.

She suppressed another stab of guilt at the expense.

It was a total indulgence, but then, given the morning she'd had, she'd more than earned it.

Tegan dropped into her chair and spun around, angling herself away from the lift doors in the unlikely event someone alighted. Apparently a very unlikely event, according to her sister. 'Invitation only' was the way she'd described this floor, and with the boss half a world away there was zero chance she'd be interrupted by anyone. Which was just the way Tegan wanted it.

She let one high-heeled court shoe drop on the carpet and lifted one knee high, curling her toes into the sheer fabric gathered between her fingers.

The stocking slipped over her toes and up her calf like a shimmering second layer of skin. She hitched up Morgan's fitted pencil-skirt and drew the stocking higher up her leg to where the lace band ended at her thigh.

Not bad, she thought, alternately flexing and pointing her toes at the ceiling in time with the music playing in her ears, liking the way the barely there stocking gave her skin a warm, golden glow, before dropping that leg down to start on the other. Maybe today wasn't going to be such a dead loss after all.

He shouldn't be watching. He hadn't intended to watch. He'd thought he heard the ping of the lift door and some vague utterances, and he'd opened his door ready to utter a few terse words himself to his recalcitrant PA. One glance at that impossibly long length of leg being sheathed in something silky, and the heat intended for his words had made a sudden change of direction and headed south.

He watched, transfixed, as her second leg followed

the first, angling upwards as she extended her knee and drew the almost invisible fabric slowly up her leg. All the long, *long* way up.

A heated breath hissed through his teeth. Who would have suspected Morgan Fielding had pins like those hidden under her 'hands off' business attire? Although she was not quite as 'hands off' as usual, he observed with a glance at the rest of her. Today the buttons at her neck were undone, exposing a rare vee of surprisingly sun-kissed skin, and the nondescript-colour hair that was usually bound into a tight knot looked more casual and sunstreaked, coiling tendrils already escaping from the clips to fall around her face and neck—no doubt due to the action of her head bopping from side to side to whatever was pumping out of the device she had plugged into her ears.

A movement had his eyes right back on her hands. Her fingers were toying with the lace tops, straightening each one slightly. *Lucky lace*, he reflected, to be wrapped around such perfect thighs.

Then he watched her run the flat of her palms along the length of each leg, smoothing the stockings from the ankle up. Not that there was any need. There wasn't so much as a wrinkle or crease to be seen from where he was standing.

They looked perfect. Legs you could slide your hand up, a smooth and silken journey northwards. Why was today so special that she'd dress her legs up in lace-topped luxury like that? Why was she suddenly flashing skin he'd never had so much of a glimpse of? It sure wasn't for his benefit.

Unless she was expecting someone in his absence.

Something ground his thoughts to a halt. Just the

thought of someone else gliding their way north along that glistening two-lane highway crunched like a bad gear-change inside him.

He drew in one long breath, but instead of the cooling effect he needed right now the oxygen-laden air merely fuelled the fire pooling in his groin, further compounding the morning's aggravation.

Damn it!

Another time, another woman, he might appreciate the rush of blood—but she was Morgan Fielding, his PA, for God's sake! And he'd never looked at Morgan Fielding that way. He didn't look at PAs period, no matter how good their attributes. Tina had cured him of that long ago.

He cleared his throat, because he knew that if he didn't his voice would come out too rough, too telling. Besides, he told himself as he pushed himself away from the door, she'd never hear him otherwise over those damned devices jammed into her ears.

'When you're quite finished…'

It took a second for her to register before he had her full attention. But that second gave birth to chaos in motion. In a moment she'd jumped out of her seat and wheeled around to face him, simultaneously pulling her skirt down to her knees while yanking the earphones free.

So he'd startled her. Good. Although he bet it was nothing compared to the shock of those endless legs he'd just been subjected to.

Then, just when he expected to meet her gaze and see her reaction get reined back to the Little Ms Efficiency she usually was—no doubt with a prim little apology for her late arrival—her look of outrage disappeared and instead her hazel eyes opened wide with shock, the colour draining clear from her face.

'You!' The word exploded from her lips like an accusation, her hands and feet combining in some crazy dance for her shoes, while her head swung between him and the lift doors, giving him the insane impression that at any moment she was planning to bolt.

'Who were you expecting?' he asked, planting his fists on her desk, only half joking. 'The Spanish Inquisition?'

She bit down on her bottom lip, battling to get her frantic heart-rate under control. Given a choice, she'd take the Spanish Inquisition over this man any day. Because she knew what James Maverick looked like. Hell, the whole of Australia and half the world besides knew what he looked like! In the last three weeks since she'd been back in the country, she'd seen one article after another featuring the corporate high-flyer sprinkled liberally from the front page, through to the deepest, darkest business pages, to the red carpet 'who's out with whom' shots.

But she also knew he wasn't supposed to be here!

'But you…' She protested from a mouth suddenly desert-dry. 'You're supposed to be in Europe. *Milan!*' she added for emphasis, as if that might make him disappear in a puff of smoke.

He leaned across the desk towards her, his rich chocolate eyes as unimpressed as they were challenging. She swallowed. She'd never thought of chocolate brown as a threatening colour, not until now; his scorching gaze seemed to suck the very air from the room. Her sister had described him as a tyrant, the A-grade boss from hell. What she hadn't told her was that he was also A-grade sex on legs. How could Morgan not have noticed? Testosterone radiated out from him like a magnetic field. He wore it as easily as his crisp blue-and-white pinstriped shirt. He wore it as easily as the mantle of power that was almost tangible around him.

And with his dark eyes and hair, and the hint of a shadowed jaw and even darker disposition, he looked for all the world like an archetypal gunslinger. It was little wonder the entire business world had dropped the 'James' years ago and simply called him Maverick. He probably had a black hat and a gun belt stashed away in his top drawer to deal with wayward clients.

Not to mention anyone masquerading as his PA.

And right now Tegan was firmly in his sights. She shivered. Had he twigged at the deception already?

'My little surprise,' he said, moving closer, a dangerous glint in his eye, and his voice a silken noose she felt tightening by the second. 'I'm very much here. Just as you are very much late and obviously not ready for work. From now on you do your head banging—and get dressed—on your own time.'

Relief the game wasn't yet up gave way to aggravation. He hadn't so much as given her an opportunity to explain why she was late.

'I was held up—'

'Obviously.'

'And I was hardly getting dressed!'

'It sure looked like it from where I was standing.'

Heat flooded back into her cheeks in outrage. 'You were watching me!'

'I was *waiting* for you,' he corrected, as if it were some kind of defence against her accusation, and he slashed one hand through the air towards her clock. 'Like I have been for the last hour and a half.'

She jagged up her chin, still incensed. 'I didn't realise it would be such a problem. It's not as if you're supposed to be here, after all.'

'It is a problem!' He rattled the words out like machine-gun fire and she drew back, knowing she'd overstepped the mark. 'And it's just as well,' he continued, 'that I refused your leave application *just in case*, because *just in case* happened. Giuseppe Zeppa had a heart attack Saturday, and as a result all negotiations with Zeppabanca are on hold indefinitely—which means placating Rogerson so he doesn't get cold feet and pull out of the Aussie end of the deal. So I suggest you get your gear organised and get into my office— and bring the Rogerson file. We've got a lot of work to get through today.'

'But…' she implored, grabbing hold of his arm before he could wheel away. *This* wasn't part of the deal. It was one thing to have him accept at face value that she was Morgan; it was another thing entirely to expect her to carry that through. She looked up at him while beneath her fingers corded power tensed, turning the muscled flesh rock-hard.

He looked down at the hand on his sleeve, and then at her, like she'd just committed some kind of major crime.

Slowly, dangerously, he angled his jaw, the cleft in his chin a menacing shadow while the look in his eyes turned to a slow, cold burn. Instantly she regretted her knee-jerk reaction. She was well and truly caught, skewered by the potent glare from his eyes.

'But what?'

The words sounded like bullets while his gaze froze her protest solid. Her hand was paralysed, still on his arm. Because what could she say—'I'm not who you think I am'? How could she admit that, other than a couple of hours of coaching as to the whys and wherefores of the job so she could at least manage the filing, she didn't really have a clue what she would be expected to do?

It took but a second to consider her options. She couldn't admit the truth. She had to try to do her best to save her sister's job, not consign it to the dustbin, which was exactly where it would go if he discovered they had switched.

And he obviously believed she was Morgan. Which was kind of amusing—Mr Hotshot-Corporate-Cowboy Maverick actually believed she was her sister! So why shouldn't he keep right on believing it—at least until she could call Morgan and get her to hightail it back here as fast as she could?

After all, she'd worked in an office before. She could type, she could operate a computer and a printer, and what Morgan hadn't filled her in on she'd learn. She dragged air into her lungs, air that came richly spiced with the heady tang of male—*angry male*—and she realised she had no choice but to do whatever it took to placate him.

She could do this for a day or two. She would do whatever it took to protect Morgan's job. And she could deal with the boss from hell in the process.

And once Morgan was home they could have a good old laugh about it.

She let go her hold on his arm and brushed a loose tendril of her hair behind her ear, doing her best to school herself into the model of efficiency he would expect. 'Of course. I'll be right there.'

CHAPTER TWO

'AND get on to Rogerson and see if you can set up a meeting for tomorrow morning at his offices.' Maverick was pacing non-stop alongside the full-length windows that overlooked the Gold Coast coastline, his hands in his pockets as he dictated his requirements. Tegan frantically scribbled, trying to keep up and make sense of his instructions.

'That's Phil Rogerson, the CEO,' she muttered half to herself, busy scratching down notes.

Maverick nodded tersely over his shoulder before continuing. 'And make sure George Huntley can be there. We'll need to work up some sort of heads of agreement.'

'From Huntley and Jacques solicitors,' she added to herself. The two minutes she'd spent frantically scanning the file before she'd joined Maverick in his office was paying far better dividends than she'd expected. It wasn't so bad. The communications to date had all been clear and succinct, and Tegan was never more grateful for Morgan's neat streak. She'd obviously had all her filing up to date before she'd finished up last week.

'And, when you've done that, I need you to arrange flowers to be sent to Giuseppe.'

'Giuseppe?' She looked up. She couldn't remember that name from the file, and yet it seemed oddly familiar.

'Giuseppe Zeppa,' he filled in. 'Find out what hospital he's in and send him the biggest and the best.'

Of course, she realised—the Italian connection who'd had the heart attack and landed her in this mess. Not that it was Giuseppe's fault. It had more to do with her sister and her crazy plans.

What had Morgan promised her? An entire week of swanning around in a plush office with nothing more to do than sort the mail and file her nails.

Tegan had known that she'd have been much more comfortable distributing food packages to queues of women and children than playing corporate PA to this guy any day—and that was before the nightmare discovery that Maverick was going to be in residence.

Only when she'd finished writing did she realise he'd stopped firing instructions at her. She raised her eyes to find him framed against the backdrop of the endless shoreline and glittering azure sea, a frown jamming his dark brows tight together.

'What's got into you today?'

She jumped. 'Nothing,' she blustered, immediately cursing the defensiveness in her tone.

He just kept on scowling at her, like he was scratching away, searching for the truth, trying to peel back the layers. She tucked a renegade strand of hair behind her ear and cocked up her chin. Attack had to be the best form of defence. 'Why do you ask?'

'Because you've been repeating everything I've said. Are you sure you're not coming down with something? Your voice sounds a little strange.'

'No! At least, not that I know of.'

'Then what the hell's wrong with you?'

'Nothing's wrong with me!'

'You've been in a strange mood all day.'

'And you've been in a bad mood all day!'

His back straightened, his hands lifting from his pockets to cross lazily over his chest. The movement was slow, languid even, but the body language was clear.

Wrong answer.

Tension lined his features, barely restrained tension that held his broad-shouldered pose rigid and forced the flicker of movement at his jaw. And suddenly it wasn't a gunslinger she was looking at. Against the glittering ocean and infinite skies he could have been a sea god, emerged from the oceans to claim the world and everything it contained. And, if he'd been holding a trident, she had no doubt it would have been launched directly at her right now.

'Is that so?' he questioned, dragging her attention back to his face and one pointedly arched brow. 'I've been in a bad mood all day?'

She swallowed. He'd probably been in that mood his entire life, if what Morgan had told her was any indication. Not that she was crazy enough to add saying that to her list of transgressions. 'At least since I got in.'

'Late.'

She cocked her head. 'Pardon?'

'You were late, I recall. Maybe if you'd got in on time you might have found my mood a little more to your liking.'

Tegan doubted it. She glanced down at her watch. How much more of this day did she have to endure?

'Expecting someone?'

She looked up at him. 'Excuse me?'

'Do you have somewhere you need to be?'

She blinked. *Where was this headed?*

'A lunch date, perhaps?'

'Not that that would be any of your business, but I'm planning on working through lunch.' She paused, knowing she should shut up now, but unable to resist giving the man back something of his own medicine. 'To make up for my earlier crimes against the state.'

Something unreadable flashed across his eyes, and his jaw worked overtime before he finally spun away to face the wall of windows. 'Good,' he said. 'That's exactly what I meant. Let me know how you get on with Rogerson.'

He even looked powerful from the back, she realised absent-mindedly, unable to miss how his shirt pulled across his broad shoulders before narrowing to tuck into a lean, packed waist and trousers that fitted in all the right places.

Suddenly he turned his head, looking back over his shoulder at her and capturing her open appraisal. His eyes narrowed, his expression remaining resolute.

'Was there something else?'

It took a second to realise she'd been dismissed and that she'd missed it completely. And, instead of running for the relative sanctuary of her work station like she should have, she'd sat here ogling him. And he'd caught her red-handed. What the hell was wrong with her, hanging around in here, when being with him was the last thing she needed?

'No,' she murmured in response as she gathered up her note pad and rose from the chair. 'Nothing at all.'

The soft snick of the catch told him she'd gone, but still he stayed where he was, watching without really seeing the endless waves roll in along the coastline.

So she didn't have a lunch date. Why had that launched such a surge of satisfaction? Why had it even mattered? She was Morgan, his PA.

His PA with the endless, smooth-skinned legs.

She'd had them tucked demurely away beneath her, but every now and then she'd shifted slightly, and those legs had shimmered in the light, drawing his eye and causing his mind to wander—and hold out for the merest glimpse of lace. Fruitlessly, as it had turned out.

So, if it wasn't a lunch date, maybe it was dinner she had planned? There had to be some reason for her less buttoned-up dress code. Unless his presence here today had spoilt some other plans she'd had in mind? That could account for the sassy attitude.

Not that he was interested. He was curious, that was all. Anything that affected the performance of a significant member of his team was a concern. And if something was bugging her he'd find out exactly what it was.

Time didn't have a chance to drag. Once back in her work space, Tegan did a more thorough once-over of the file to assure herself she was on the right track, before launching into the myriad tasks Maverick had set her, all the time praying she didn't make any major blunders.

But, before any of that, the first thing she'd done was to take the time to email Morgan in Honolulu. *Urgent*, she'd written in the subject header. *Call me tonight at home asap!*

She could only hope Morgan would check her private email daily, as she'd promised when Tegan had agreed to this crazy scheme.

Not that she'd really agreed to anything, when it all came down to it. She'd been well and truly guilt-tripped into it.

'You owe me,' Morgan had pleaded. 'When Dad was sick I had to use up all my leave to look after him.'

'I had a fever!' Tegan had argued. 'I wanted to come home, you know that, but they wouldn't let me travel.'

Morgan had been unsympathetic. 'It doesn't change the fact I had to look after him by myself. Now I've got no leave left, and Maverick insists I sit at my desk all week just in case he wants me to send a fax somewhere. Come on, Tegan, it's the least you can do. Bryony is my best friend, and the wedding's only two weeks away. How can I tell her at this stage that I can't be her chief bridesmaid?'

'But nobody is going to believe I'm you for an entire week.'

'Why not? Maverick will be half a world away, and anybody that knows I have a sister thinks she's still off fighting the good cause in some Third World country somewhere.'

Half a world away. If only.

Tegan had tried to find holes in her sister's scheme, had tried to find where it could fall down. She sighed as she remembered the countless arguments, the many 'what if's as she'd argued her case and why it couldn't work. But her twin had been convincing, in spite of Tegan's doubts—'a piece of cake', she'd called it. She'd made it sound doable. She'd even managed at times to make it sound logical. Besides, how else would Morgan have been able to get to Bryony's wedding? Morgan's boss could not have been allowed to get away with such a mean gesture.

Besides, Morgan had been right about one thing: Tegan owed her sister big time for caring for their father after his sudden stroke, when Tegan had been able to do no more than worry from a distance. In the end, battling against a mystery virus in a dusty African camp hospital, she'd heard the chilling news that her father had suffered another stroke, this time fatal. It was two months before she'd been declared fit enough to travel, too late to see her father one last time, and two months too late to help Morgan.

So, yes, Tegan owed her. And Morgan had made it sound foolproof. Except that neither of them had once considered the possibility that the Italian trip wouldn't go ahead.

Maverick was here…

And so what that he'd been taken in today; how long could she maintain the deception? Morgan would just have to come home, and the sooner the better. There was nothing else for it.

'You look deep in thought.'

She jumped at his voice, looking up in panic, hoping the scattered contents of files and paperwork on her desk didn't betray too much of her inexperience.

If it did, he didn't comment. He dropped a stack of files topped with a pile of paperwork onto a relatively uncluttered part of her desk.

'What's the latest with Phil?'

She schooled her face into something she hoped was approaching coolly professional. 'I'm just awaiting final confirmation he can make it for ten tomorrow—

the lawyers look like falling in if that's a goer. It shouldn't be too long now.'

'Good. I'll be out talking to our finance people,' he said, heading towards the lifts. 'I might be late.'

'What do you want me to do with these?' she called out behind him, indicating the stack of material he'd left behind.

He turned, a small furrow marring his noble brow. 'Exactly what you normally do with them. Is there a problem with that?'

She plastered a bright and hopefully not too false smile on her face. 'I thought as much,' she lied, before the scowling personage disappeared into the lift. 'Just checking.'

He needed a cold beer. If the meeting with a bunch of dry and dusty finance people hadn't been enough, a trip past his grandmother's nursing home had certainly given him a thirst. The old lady sure wasn't getting any easier. Some days she welcomed him like she'd always done, and was full of bright stories about growing up on the family ranch in Montana. And other times she just seemed determined to give him a hard time.

This afternoon had been one of those times.

The lift hummed quietly up through the floors towards his office suite as he tugged loose his tie and undid his top button.

On the way back from the private nursing-home he'd toyed with the idea of calling up someone from his current list of contacts to see if they were interested in going out for dinner, but in the end he'd decided against it. People knew he was supposed to be overseas this week, and somehow a meaningless dinner for the hell of it seemed just that—meaningless. Besides, he hadn't wanted to give any of his current female companions a reason to think she'd been singled out for special treatment, when all he'd wanted to do was avoid eating alone.

Eating alone was still preferable to being devoured alive.

So he'd grab a few files from the office and pick up some Chinese takeaway on the way home, where he could enjoy that beer while he prepared for tomorrow's round of meetings. Rogerson had been shaky on the deal before Giuseppe's collapse had put their negotiations on hold. He mustn't be allowed to get cold feet now.

The lift doors opened to a still brightly lit office-lobby. Vaguely he registered that the cleaners must be late in servicing the floor, but his mind was still busy anticipating the beer. It had been a frustrating few days, today especially.

Then a filing-cabinet door slammed and the cause of much of today's frustrations popped her head up behind it.

'Oh,' she said, her hazel eyes wide as she quickly removed her earphones and wound them around her iPod. 'I didn't hear you come in.'

'No doubt due to that thing you had stuck in your ears again.'

'I only just turned it on! It was so quiet here.'

'What are you doing here, anyway?' His voice came out gruffer than expected, but he couldn't help it. Morgan Fielding had played no part in his plans for a quiet evening. Frankly, he didn't need the aggravation.

And he really didn't care one way or the other about

her MP3 player, other than that if she hadn't been wearing it this morning she might have heard him approaching and saved him from being subjected to that chorus-girl display of leg. A display of leg that had worked its way into his thoughts at all sorts of inopportune times today, and had raised all sorts of questions— like if the legs hidden under her give-nothing-away skirts looked that good, then what about the rest of her, covered by those 'take no prisoners' buttoned-up shirts and jackets she hid herself behind?

What other treasures lay beneath the severe suits, waiting to be revealed?

Her back stiffened as if she'd read his thoughts, her hazel eyes flashing green-tinged sparks. 'I work here.'

He moved closer, intrigued by the phenomenon. It was something he'd never noticed before, and they'd been working together at least a year and a half. How had he never noticed the way her eyes flared before now? Or was it related to her mood? Her temper had certainly flared more than he'd ever noticed before.

'I thought you would have gone home by now.'

'I got in late, remember?' Eyelids dropped down like shutters over her eyes. 'I was making up for your precious lost time.' Her mouth closed on a pout, a full bottom lip supporting a Cupid's bow that still managed to look lush and inviting even while striking that haughty pose.

She had great lips. Great lips and sensational legs, and eyes that sparked like fireworks, and there was no way he didn't want to get closer to see what other features Morgan Fielding had been concealing up till now.

Studiously ignoring him, she tilted her head away

and picked up another piece of paper from the pile next to her, looked it over briefly, and dragged open the top drawer of the cabinet, her fingers searching through for the correct file.

'You already worked through lunch,' he said, edging closer until he was alongside her as she selected a file and slipped the paperwork in. He caught a whiff of her scent as she moved, and he drank it in like fine wine. Whatever it was, it suited her—warm and womanly and evocative. *And definitely not subtle.*

He leaned one arm up on the filing cabinet next to where she was working and studied her. Her hair was different too. Normally it didn't move all day, but today it had refused to be imprisoned from the start, and the course of a few hours had further relaxed it. He liked the way it escaped in tiny curling tendrils that seemed to shine in a dozen colours, from dark blond through to sun gold. 'You don't eat?'

'I was very late. Unforgivably so, apparently. I figured me taking time out to eat was a luxury the company could ill afford.'

He noticed she didn't look at him. He also noticed the colour was rising in her cheeks. With anger? Although, she didn't seem angry, more *bothered* by his proximity. What did she think he was going to do? She was his PA, for heaven's sake.

She replaced the file in the cabinet but it was Maverick who caught the drawer and pushed it closed.

She looked up at him. 'What are you doing? I haven't finished.'

'And just what do you think *you're* doing?'

'What does it look like I'm doing?' she snapped. 'I'm taking a bath!'

He blinked, the mental picture that comment suddenly evoked too much to digest. A bath and those legs—now there was a heady combination. Even better, someone would have to peel down those stockings for her first. Breath whistled through his teeth while once again fire flared into life in his groin. A damn shame she was his PA. A damn shame.

Otherwise he just might have been tempted to do something stupid, like move even closer and see if that sassy mouth was as generous in the kissing department as it was in the giving lip department.

'A bath,' he murmured, crossing his arms. Mentally he shifted beer to his number-two favourite thing right now. 'Now there's a thought after a long day.'

He caught the flash of fear in her eyes. He also caught something else there too—a tiny tremor that had her lips parting as she gave a tiny, almost breathless gasp—and a tiny pause when her eyes rested on his lips before they slid away to the lift as if it were some kind of lifeline.

'I'm sorry,' she said. 'I shouldn't have said that. I was just finishing off the filing before I went home.'

He frowned, at both her words and her suddenly skittish nature after she'd been so feisty before. Did she really think he was planning to carry her off to the bathroom in his suite here and now? And why should that be a problem, even if he was? Most women he knew would welcome the suggestion. 'You told me you always prefer to do your filing first thing in the morning, while you're fresh. I thought you hated doing it in the evening.'

'Ah, well…' Now she looked even more trapped, like someone had sprung a snare on her. 'Usually I do, that's true. But seeing I was making up some time I thought I might as well make an early start with it, given tomorrow's set to be a big day.' She edged away, giving him a wide berth as she circled around to her desk. He got the impression she was fleeing. 'I should get going,' she whispered, confirming his thoughts, a husky layer in her voice grating on his senses.

He watched her close down her computer before slipping on her navy jacket and gathering up her bag, stuffing her bright-pink iPod into a pocket.

'By the way,' she said without looking up, 'Phil Rogerson's confirmed for ten a.m., and the lawyers have rescheduled so they can be there. It's all set. Good night. I'll see you in the morning.'

She was halfway to the lift when the truth hit him. Tonight he had no interest in eating alone. Tonight he'd rather spend time going a few more rounds with this challenge of a female—all executive finesse one day, all paradoxical woman the next.

'Morgan!'

She stopped, and he saw her back straighten as she took a breath before turning slowly around.

'Yes?'

'Have dinner with me.'

CHAPTER THREE

SHE blinked once, a slow-motion shutter over her suddenly expressive eyes. Then she gave a barely there shake of her head. 'No.' She turned abruptly around and bridged the remaining distance to the lift, making sure not to press the down button too lightly to register. In fact it was a wonder she didn't push the button clear through the wall.

There was the sound of movement behind her, pounding feet across the floor, and then the steel grip of his large hand wrapping like a manacle around her wrist and forcing her around. 'That's it?' he questioned. 'Just "no"?'

Even through her jacket his touch felt like a brand, scorching and searing its way deep into her flesh, bone-melting heat that threatened her resolve to get out of here as quickly as she could.

She looked down at the hand circling her wrist, so large and masculine against her navy jacket. Just a few hours ago it had been her hand on his arm, trying to stop him, when her worst nightmare had happened and she'd realised she was stuck in this pretence until Morgan returned. But this time he was trying to stop her.

How the tables had turned.

She raised her eyes slowly, determined that he wouldn't see how much his touch affected her. 'What's wrong?' she challenged. 'Not used to getting no for an answer?'

'You're meeting someone.'

She wanted to laugh at his knee-jerk reaction. Of course a man like Maverick would assume a woman would feel incomplete without a male, especially when offered his scintillating company. But she didn't laugh—she couldn't—not given the way the heat radiating from his eyes paralleled that from his grip, setting her skin to a tingling mess of nerve endings. Instead she battled to get her racing pulse under control, to get her breathing more regular, while wondering if she should compound her sins by inventing a boyfriend Morgan would have to conveniently shed upon her return.

In the end she merely shook her head. The lie was big enough, and getting bigger without her adding to it.

'Then why not eat with me?'

'I don't think it's a good idea.'

'You haven't eaten all day.'

Somewhere along the line he'd relaxed the tone of his voice. It was less strident, more persuasive. And somewhere along the line he'd also relaxed his hold on her wrist, so that his thumb stroked the underside of her wrist, making lazy circles on her skin. Lazy circles, to counteract a frantic pulse. It was hypnotising, so gentle in comparison to his cast-iron grip of before, but no less bone-sappingly heat generating. Warmth bloomed like soft sunlight throughout her body, warming her breasts to tingling, before pooling heavy and insistent between her thighs.

She swallowed, not sure she could trust herself to speak. 'I had an apple.'

The corners of his mouth curled while his body hovered too close, too hard and too hot.

'Tempting,' he acknowledged, still stroking her arm, the circles larger now. 'But hardly enough.'

'I'll eat when I get home.'

'I'll take you home after we've eaten.'

'I told you, it's not a good idea.'

'Why not?'

Because I'm not who you think I am, she wanted to shout. *Because it will only complicate things when Morgan returns.*

She sighed, struggling to find the right answer, because things were far, far too complicated already.

'Because I don't want to!' she finally settled for. 'And you can't make me.'

His eyes narrowed. 'It's only a meal.'

Was it? The words themselves sounded perfectly logical, and yet when did 'only a meal' invitations come with a heated massage of her wrist and her senses? When did they come with dark eyes that simmered like melted chocolate, looking like they were ready to suck her down into so much molten bliss, so much so that the concept of eating a meal morphed into visions of much more carnal delights? And, if he could make her burn with just one look, with just one touch, then what more was possible?

Oh God, she had to get out of here, before she started wanting to find out.

'I want to go,' she stated as emphatically as she could, hoping her voice sounded convincing when every other part of her was insanely drawn to him, insanely drawn to what she knew would be more dangerous than stepping into quicksand. Somehow she knew that once those eyes had sucked her in there would be no escape.

It couldn't be allowed to happen!

As if on cue, the lift pinged, announcing its arrival, the doors sliding open alongside her. Escape! She turned away from him, turned away from his heat and towards the welcoming cave of the lift where the air already seemed cooler. Safer.

She wrenched her arm away, assuming she would meet with resistance to her dash for freedom, but there was none, and the momentum of jerking her arm caught her wrong-footed and sent her tripping sideways towards the lift door-frame.

She cried out, trying simultaneously to regain her footing and brace herself for the impact to come, when he caught her in a tangle of feet and arms and spun her into his arms. Her chest collided with his, which sent the air in her lungs whooshing out of her. But she was saved. She dragged in air, content for the moment to rest in the circle of his arms, his lean body lending her strength while she caught her breath.

'Okay now?' he murmured in her ear, his cheek pressed against her hair and his warm breath a silken caress.

She drew in another long breath, feeling the beat of her heart slow and regulate before she felt steady enough to respond.

'Th…thank you,' she whispered, finally feeling confident enough to try to push herself away. She raised her hands to his chest and felt the answering thud of his own heartbeat. And in the space of just a second or two she felt it kick up a notch, a double-barrelled call to arms.

The relief that she hadn't crash-landed gave way to a fear that she'd been saved into circumstances much more dangerous indeed.

She edged back and looked up at him, and felt the connection with his eyes like a bolt of electricity. They were so dark, so heavy with desire—*desire for her*.

No, she registered from some far-off place. Not for *her*.

He thought she was Morgan.

It was Morgan he took her for. It was Morgan he wanted.

But right now that didn't seem to matter, not with the way his eyes focused on her mouth, not with the way his lips hovered so tantalisingly close to her own.

He might think she was Morgan, but it was Tegan he was going to kiss.

And it was Tegan who was going to let him.

With one hand he lifted her chin, and her lips parted on a sigh.

His answering growl fed into her senses like a rolling wave of desire, and she barely registered the lift doors sliding closed behind her, cutting off her escape route.

Except escape was now the furthest thing from her mind, and, just when she thought it wasn't possible to feel any more, he kissed her. One brief touch at first, then a second that was more an intermingling of breath, a sampling, an introduction, and then he came back, increasing the pressure as he pressed his lips to her own. His were a revelation—firm and yet gentle, masterful without dominating. Instead they gave generously, inviting her to participate in the dance of lips, and then, as he deepened the kiss, tongues.

And it was no hardship at all to accept his invitation.

Her spine seemed to melt, her body arching into his, letting herself be supported by his hands, while she clung to him, wrapping her arms around his neck and pulling him close, feeding on his male taste and touch even as he supped on her.

Such wide shoulders, such lean, muscled flesh; her hands relished the sculpted skinscape of him. She curled her fingers into the shirt covering his firm flesh, feeling his muscles flex and tighten beneath. He shuddered when she raked her nails across the fine fabric, and pressed his long, lean length closer to her so she could not be in any way ignorant to the extent of his arousal.

How empowering. Knowing she could do this to him. Knowing that a man like Maverick would react to her touch. Knowing that a man like Maverick wanted her.

His hand scooped its way under her jacket, sweeping the length of her back, setting her skin alight in a sensual massage. *This man came with heat,* she realised, answering an earlier question. Everywhere he touched her burned. Everywhere he touched her sizzled.

It was Maverick setting her aflame.

She was crazy, she recognised; she must be crazy. But it was the kind of crazy that rolled you into a ball and kept you moving, without a chance of drawing breath, without a chance of finding your feet and coming up for air. And as she drank his male essence into her senses she had to admit there was definitely something to be said for being crazy.

He tilted his head and directed his mouth down the line of her jaw and her throat, his hands moving over her back, his fingers and thumbs seeming to test every part of her flesh, but, she had no doubt, giving much more than they were receiving.

His fingers rounded her rib cage and brushed the underswell of her breast. She gasped, arching involuntarily into the movement, and momentarily lost in sensations so foreign to her and yet at the same time so evocative. It was like a drug, this feeling coursing through her, feelings that simultaneously made her senses sing and turned logic fuzzy. It had taken but one kiss and she was addicted.

He cupped one breast with his hand, brushing her nipple with his thumb. Air rushed into her lungs like he'd switched on a vacuum, and the addict in her craved more.

He trailed kisses along her jaw, burying his face in her hair and breathing her in.

'You've driven me crazy all day, you know that?'

The whispered words rumbled through her. If she could have strung two words together right now it would have been to tell him the feeling was entirely mutual. But then he returned his attentions to her mouth, and words seemed unnecessary when her lips could tell him so much more effectively.

He groaned into her mouth and dragged his head back.

'Do you realise how much I want you?'

A tremor shimmied through her. And a flicker of fear. Through the drug-inducing haze of sensation, she recognised this wasn't a good idea. Things had gone too far—too fast—and a kiss had turned into something else entirely.

'Maverick…'

'Stay with me,' he murmured, his voice husky, his breathing choppy. 'Here in my suite. Tonight.'

It was insane, but for a moment she was actually tempted—to feel more of this exquisite rush, to experience more of what he obviously had to offer. But it was madness.

'I don't think—'

'Don't think!' he urged. 'Just feel. Make love with me tonight, Morgan. All night.'

Morgan!

Her sister's name was a chilling wave more effective than a bucket of iced water, dousing her cold. He thought he was kissing Morgan. He *expected* to make love to Morgan! And Tegan was already living a lie. How could she compound it by sleeping with him and letting him think all the time she was her sister?

She couldn't do it. Casual sex had never been her style, and this wouldn't be casual sex, anyway. It would be highly complicated, 'look out for the fallout' kind of sex.

She didn't need it, and she was pretty certain Morgan would thank her for making that decision.

'I really have to go,' she protested, simultaneously trying to push him away with one hand and clamour with the other for the button on the wall somewhere behind her that would be her ticket to freedom.

The swirling depths of his eyes revealed his confusion. 'But you don't want to go,' he responded, loosening his hold without letting her go completely. 'Not from the way your body responds.'

'I *have* to go!' she insisted, using the slight freedom he'd afforded her to find the control panel and slam her fingers against anything remotely button-shaped. 'I'm expecting a call.'

It was the truth, though the look he gave her showed he assumed it was merely an excuse to get out of there. His eyes iced over and he let her go. 'You should have said,' he stated, his voice back to business, all trace of the husky seducer banished. 'Come on, then, I'll drive you home.'

'No,' she said, holding up one hand to his chest, not wanting to risk being in this man's company any longer than she had to. The way he'd impacted upon her tonight showed her she couldn't trust herself. 'There's no need.'

'We can talk.'

'We have nothing to talk about!'

The line of his jaw hardened, and the confusion she'd seen earlier in his eyes turned a deep shade of bitter. 'So, you run.'

The lift doors pinged behind her, and without taking her eyes from his she positioned herself closer so that this time when the doors opened she'd be far enough away from him that there'd be no chance she'd be wrong-footed.

'I told you having dinner together was a bad idea. What happened just now was an even worse one.'

The doors slid open behind her and she made for the welcoming depths, punching the ground floor and close buttons simultaneously. They still took too long, and it seemed an eternity before it was just the memory of his damning scowl and open-footed gunslinger stance that had threatened to buckle her knees.

Sanity returned to Maverick with the closing of the doors. Sanity and fury. What the hell had he been thinking? She was his PA, for heaven's sake. How could a couple of long legs and hazel eyes have made him suddenly and so easily forget that?

He tugged on his tie and wheeled around. Not just long legs, though. Sensational legs. And eyes that seemed to peer right inside him. What had they seen? What was it that had made her flee like the demons of hell were after her?

Damn it, but he was determined to find out.

The phone was ringing when she entered the flat. She threw keys and bag to one side and dived for the phone in the same rapid motion.

'Morgan!' she cried into the receiver.

There was a pause.

'Is that you, Morgan?'

Tegan's heart skipped a beat as she screwed her face into a silent scream. What had she just done?

'Maverick. Why are you calling?'

'Is something wrong?'

'I just got in. I'm just a bit breathless.' She collapsed into an armchair and held on tight, praying he would accept her explanation.

'You've only just got home? You should have let me drive you.'

Tegan let go a sigh of relief. It made sense that someone like Maverick wouldn't have a clue how long it took to get anywhere when you relied on public transport.

'I didn't want you to. Was there something you wanted?'

There was a pause. 'Just to make sure you made it home all right.'

'I'm home. I'm safe,' she said, feeling one hell of a lot safer now that she was away from him.

'Look, Morgan, about what happened—'

'Thanks for calling,' she said with false brightness. 'But, if it's all the same to you, I'd rather forget what happened.' And she terminated the call.

Nobody hung up on Maverick. Not company directors or corporate wheeler-dealers or any of his women friends. And least of all his own PA. He fought back the urge to call right back and tell Miss Sassy Mouth exactly that, but he hadn't got to where he was in business by necessarily acting on his first flush of fury.

Besides, maybe she was doing him a favour. She was his PA, after all. He didn't do PAs. His self-imposed rule that he never got involved with a member of his staff was there for a very good reason.

Bitterness rose up like bile in his throat. How anyone could have done what Tina had done…

But, given that she had, he should have known better and left Morgan well enough alone.

He dragged air into lungs that had seen one hell of a crazy weekend. A flight to Milan on Saturday to conclude their deal, only to have the entire journey aborted halfway at the sad news of Giuseppe's collapse, and his return to Australia on the first available flight. Since then he'd been embroiled in planning the nego-tiations necessary to shore up the inroads they had made, all of which had been compounded by the added aggravation of a PA who seemed to have undergone a personality transplant.

Tomorrow things would be back to normal. He'd see to the Rogerson deal and ensure that the one loose end of the deal was tied up, in preparation for when Zeppabanca was ready to proceed once again.

And by tomorrow Morgan might have slept off

whatever strange affliction had affected her today and be back to her normal self, so he could concentrate on work without the constant distractions. He could hardly wait.

CHAPTER FOUR

'HEY, Tiggy! How's it going?'

Tegan breathed a sigh of relief at her sister's familiar greeting. She'd approached the ringing phone with a mixture of trepidation and fear, picking it up warily, and not game this time to second guess who the caller was. She wasn't making that mistake again.

'Morgan, it's a disaster. You have to get back here right away.'

'Why, what's wrong?'

'Maverick, that's what's wrong.'

A split second of silence answered the announcement. 'What do you mean? He's in Milan all week. How can he be a problem?'

'Giuseppe Zeppa had a heart attack. The Zeppabanca deal is on ice, at least for the time being. Maverick is here.'

'Oh, hell. So what happened?'

'I told you, it's a total disaster. You have to come back straight away.'

'You mean he knows?'

'He knows something isn't right.'

Another pause.

'But he doesn't actually *know* you're not me?'

'Not yet, but he's here. Isn't that bad enough? I can't do this, Morgan. It was a crazy enough plan to pretend to be you when he was away, but now that Maverick's here it's impossible!'

'But Bryony's wedding is tomorrow! I can't leave now.'

'So why does she have to get married on a Tuesday, anyway—and all the way over in Hawaii? Why couldn't she just get married at her local church like any normal person?'

'You've met Bryony. She just likes to be different. It's going to be a gorgeous wedding. I really want to thank you for doing this for me so I can be here for it.'

'Stop thanking me! You can't abandon me like this—not with Maverick here. There's no way it will work.'

'Hey, you promised me, remember?'

'But that was before—and you know I was never happy about the idea anyway. But now it's hopeless. You have to come back, don't you see?'

There was silence at the other end of the line. 'Morgan?'

'Sorry, sis, I was thinking. Look, even if I did manage to get a ticket and leave on the first flight tomorrow, then I still wouldn't make it back to work before Wednesday…'

'And?'

'And that means you'll have been working with him for two days already by then.'

'Which is two days too long!'

'But the chances are, if he didn't twig to our switch today, then…'

Panic flared in Tegan's gut. 'And what makes you think he won't twig to it tomorrow?'

'Look, it makes sense. If you made it through today with him convinced you were me, then he'll just assume it's business as usual tomorrow.'

'But in any case you'll be back the next day, then?'

'Well, I kind of figure that if you can make it through two days in the job you'll be a shoe-in for the week.'

'No! You don't understand. I can't work with him.'

'I know he can be difficult, but I know you—you can do it.'

'Morgan, it's not exactly the work I'm worried about.'

Tegan coiled the phone cord around her finger nervously while she waited for her sister to respond.

'What do you mean?' Morgan said at last.

'Listen, I know you've always referred to him as the boss from hell, so this may seem like a silly question, but has Maverick ever tried to come on to you?'

Unrestrained laughter met her question. 'You must be kidding! The kind of woman Maverick goes for socially is hardly his PA. He made that plain when I took the job. "Don't get ideas," he told me flat at the interview. "Because you'll be out of here on your ear before you know it." And that suits me fine. He's really not my type.'

But that made no sense, Tegan reasoned. Maverick had been coming on to Morgan tonight—hadn't he?

'So, you mean he's never shown any interest in you?'

'Of course not. What's happened, Tiggy, do you think he made a pass at you or something?'

Tegan winced. Normally she'd tell her sister everything, but there was no way she was about to confess to everything that had happened tonight. 'Well, maybe something like that.'

'Then forget it. Maverick isn't like that. It's one of

his mantras. *Don't mess with the PA.* Apparently it happened once before and ended badly, and he's never forgiven the woman. And he's made sure he's never let himself get into the same position. So don't worry. Whatever it is, you've probably just blown it out of all proportion.'

If only. But, then again, if what Morgan said was right maybe Maverick was already regretting that kiss. Maybe that was why he'd rung—to apologise and to promise her it wouldn't happen again. *And she'd all but hung up on him.* Tegan squeezed her eyes shut at the memory. Well, at any rate, that would help convince him he'd been right not to mess with his staff.

Tegan let her sister prattle on about the wedding plans and the weather and the gorgeous scenery. She had to admit she couldn't in all honesty begrudge her sister the good time. Morgan deserved it, after all she'd done to look after their father in his last months. When she hadn't been working flat out for Maverick, she'd been helping their father. She'd shut herself off from the world and she deserved this chance for a break.

If only Maverick had been able to see that, and had approved Morgan's request for leave, it would have saved them all some grief.

Tegan was already at work the next day when Maverick arrived. She flicked him no more than a frosty glance, with a cool 'Good morning' to keep it company, and continued typing up what looked like the agenda for this morning's meeting that he'd left on her desk last night.

Likewise he didn't hesitate as he breezed past her into his office. She might want to pretend that kiss last night had never happened, but he'd already forgotten about it.

He threw himself into his chair, took one look at his desk and swung his chair around so he faced the golden strip of beach and sapphire sea instead. He was still there when there was a knock on the door ten minutes later.

'Sorry, am I interrupting?'

He swung around and let go a gruff 'No,' designed to sound like a 'yes'.

'That agenda you wanted,' she said, approaching his desk without looking at him. 'And the mail.'

Today she had on another of those God-awful suits again, this time some bland coffee colour. It was probably a decent suit, except that it somehow managed to disguise every curve he knew was hidden away underneath. *Knew*, because he'd had a taste of them last night.

She dropped the papers on his desk and turned, and he almost growled. Even the back view gave nothing away. His gaze lowered, and he felt his brow knit into a frown. So she'd dispensed with her experiment with lace-topped nothingness and reverted to the heavy-artillery leg camouflage. It was unnecessary, given he wasn't interested, but probably a wise move. At least she wouldn't inadvertently provide any distractions during their meetings today.

'Morgan,' he said, leaning forward in his chair to pick up the prepared agenda.

She stilled at the door and half turned, staring at a spot on the floor. 'Yes?'

'Make sure Rogerson's people get a copy of this before the meeting,' he said, holding up the agenda.

'And I'll need you at the meeting to take minutes. I'll be leaving in an hour. Can you be ready?'

Her eyes lifted, frosted cola and lime that should have chilled him to the core, but only served to make his blood boil long after she'd snipped out a single 'Fine' and left the room.

It was good she was back to something approaching what he expected of her in terms of her efficiency, but she couldn't have given him a clearer or louder 'hands off' signal. And did she really think that was entirely necessary? Did she really think he was going to come anywhere near her again after what had happened?

Not likely!

'Rogerson's a tough old bird,' Maverick explained while he negotiated his obsidian-black Mercedes SLK convertible north along the Gold Coast Highway. 'Very old-school. He was nervous about the deal before Giuseppe's collapse. Now he's liable to back out completely if we don't offer some assurance that the deal will go ahead.'

Tegan took Maverick's explanation to mean that Morgan and Rogerson had never met. As it was, she could hardly ask. She'd spent much of yesterday explaining why she was doing things differently. Today she was determined to show him that the old Morgan he knew was back in business.

So she pressed herself back in the luxurious leather upholstery, surrounded by the type of man-toy extravagance she'd forever associate with this man. She tried hard to ignore the smell of fine leather which combined with Maverick's signature scent into a heady combination featuring key notes of power, wealth and testosterone, intoxicating characteristics that wound their way into her psyche despite her best efforts. Beguiling. Alluring. *Dangerous.*

But he would not affect her; she wouldn't let him. Today was back to business, pure and simple. And, from his behaviour so far, Maverick was in total agreement with her on that.

'So what happens if Rogerson won't play ball?' she asked, looking out the window so she didn't have to be reminded of the way his trousers moulded to the lean muscled length of his legs. 'Or he does, and the worst happens and the Zeppabanca deal never gets off the ground?'

He smoothly changed lanes and overtook another vehicle. 'It will go ahead, I have no doubt. But Rogerson had another two parties courting them with major building proposals before I put this deal with Zeppabanca to them. Those parties would be only too happy to have a second bite at the cherry and sign him up now. That's what we have to act to prevent today—to ensure Rogerson is still in place for when we do go ahead.'

'But surely he needs you more than you need him? There are plenty of other builders out there.'

'True, but I don't want them. I want Rogerson. I trust him. He may be conservative, but he's unscrupulously honest, and in this business that's worth more than gold. Plus he builds to quality, not to a price, so there'll be no risk of him cost cutting in an attempt to improve his margin. And that's the kind of partner we need. Royalty Cove is going to be the Gold Coast's sovereign building development of the decade. It has to be done properly.'

He steered the car off the main road into a side street lined with medium-sized office buildings, pulling into a car park behind one bearing the signage of *Rogerson Developments*.

'Very modest,' she said, climbing from the car, noting the difference between this industrial estate and the glittering high rise that made up the centre of the Gold Coast business precinct.

'That's Phil Rogerson for you. You'd never know he was a multi-millionaire in his own right.'

And she wouldn't have picked it either, when a few minutes later she was led into a boardroom headed by a wiry grey-haired man wearing a battered blue cardigan that had seen better days. His high leathery brow was criss-crossed with a deep pattern that bore witness to years of frowning on building sites under the hot Queensland sun, and his broad nose and bushy eyebrows screamed character. It was only the piercing blue eyes that suggested this man wasn't as old or as past it as he first seemed. And there was something else that perplexed her, a familiarity with his features, something that immediately had her mind searching for answers even though she was almost certain she'd never met him before.

He wrapped her hand in his own large, callused version and welcomed her to the meeting, his beaming smile deepening the grooves arcing from his nose to the corners of his mouth and beyond.

'Delighted to meet you at last,' he told her. 'Maverick seems to have you permanently chained to that office. Though now I can see why. I'm glad we gave him the opportunity to set you free at last.'

When the older man smiled, his weathered face

dropped about ten years, and he looked more like a young granddad than the sun-dried successful builder he was. She couldn't help but smile back, and not only because he'd just put her mind at rest over whether Morgan had ever met him. Though it didn't go anywhere near solving the mystery of why he should look somewhat familiar.

The lawyers arrived along with Maverick's team of finance people, and in the next few minutes the various teams were introduced and settled around the long board-table, jugs of water and a tray of glasses jostling for space between the stacks of papers.

Tegan found herself seated alongside Maverick at one end of the table with Phil Rogerson at the other, but even with a dozen or so others present it was like being trapped in the car with him all over again. It was his aura that surrounded her, it was his heat that turned her own thermostat on to a slow burn. And his legs seemed to be everywhere under the table, impossibly long, impossibly restless, several times brushing against hers, until the only way she could avoid contact was to jam her legs tightly around the chair leg farthest from him.

The lawyers opened the meeting, talking for some length about the situation—detailing and spelling out the legal implications that, since the Zeppabanca deal hadn't been completed by the prescribed date, any and all understandings between the parties were no longer binding. The parties were now legally free agents.

It was then Maverick's turn to speak. After highlighting the major points of the project, and the benefits that would flow to each of the three partners, he concluded, 'Royalty Cove has to go ahead.' He slammed a fist into his hand. 'This is the premier property development for the Gold Coast for the next decade and beyond. We have an opportunity to undertake the most prestigious and yet environmentally low-impact development ever, and show the rest of Australia and indeed the world how it's done in the process.

'The only way we can achieve that is if we start with the best team in the business—because Royalty Cove deserves the best. Royalty Cove demands the best. Which is why we need Rogerson Developments on board. Quite simply, nobody builds better properties of the kind we're talking about. But we have to be prepared to move as soon as Zeppabanca is back in business. And we need to be prepared to commit now.'

There was something about his voice, Tegan realised, a confidence in those low tones that pulled you along with him, and that made you listen and believe what he was saying must be right. Even now several others around the table were nodding their agreement. It was no wonder he'd reached the dizzy heights he had in business. But he wasn't getting it all his own way. At the other end of the table she could see Phil Rogerson was still wavering as he peered down the table over his steepled fingers.

'There's no mistaking the concept has merit,' he began cautiously, and Tegan sensed the man beside her stiffen. 'And I can feel the passion you have for the project. But, given the Giuseppe Zeppa situation, how can we be sure Zeppabanca will want to continue their part in the deal?'

'Giuseppe was right behind the project from the start.'

'But if he has to stand down, or should the worst happen…' Rogerson held up his hands in a shrug and nobody was in doubt as to what that worst might be.

'What if their next CEO isn't enthusiastic, or wants to reconsider? You have to understand my position. I can't afford to be tied into an uncertainty that locks me out of other opportunities. You were aware I had two other partnership proposals on my desk—well, just this morning I received a third, and this one starts in less than three months. I'll have guaranteed employment for my teams for the next three years.'

'The Royalty Cove deal will see them busy for at least seven!'

'But may not go ahead.'

'It *will* go ahead. And to be the best Royalty Cove needs Rogerson Developments on board. There's no question of that.'

'And, if it does, then when will it happen?' He sighed. 'I'm afraid I think I'd need an assurance from Zeppabanca that they're going to be party to this deal.'

'You know Giuseppe is ill. I can't give you that.'

'I realise that. So maybe we've all been wasting our time.'

'Then I will give you my personal guarantee!'

Every head swung around in surprise.

'What do you mean?' Rogerson asked, his eyes narrowed into slits. 'Your "personal guarantee"?'

All eyes turned to Maverick for the answer to the question on everyone's lips.

'Simply this. That if concerns about your teams lying idle for any time are stopping you from committing to Royalty Cove, then I'll take that concern right away. I'll cover your teams for any losses they make or any delays while we wait for news on Zeppabanca. You won't be out of pocket, and more importantly they won't be out of a job. Nobody will lose.'

Tegan watched the interplay between the two men, both of them successful, both of them leaders, and yet one risk averse, the other a risk taker. Now Maverick was not merely putting his support behind the project, he was backing it with cold, hard cash, and plenty of it.

Rogerson finally arched one heavily forested eyebrow and grunted, and with that gesture Tegan instantly felt herself transported back to the refugee camp in Somalia, tending a line of women and children waiting to see the visiting *Médecin Sans Frontières* team. And at the head of the queue, sitting on a camp stool while he tended a crying baby, while its hollow-eyed mother watched on hopelessly, had been a late-thirties man with wild hair and bushy eyebrows who'd made the kids laugh when he'd cocked one up high and then waggled them. Everyone had simply referred to him as Dr Sam, but his surname had been Rogerson, she was sure. And the resemblance was all too suddenly unmistakeable.

'I think we should break for coffee and consider this latest development,' Rogerson went on to say. He looked at his watch. 'Fifteen-minute break, everyone.'

Pots of filtered coffee and jugs of orange juice appeared on a side table, along with plates of cookies and tiny sandwiches.

Several of the legal team came to talk to Maverick, and Tegan noticed Rogerson being similarly besieged at the other end of the table. She eased away to pour Maverick a coffee and grab herself a juice, wondering if she'd get the chance to talk to Phil at all and ask him about the connection when in fact it was Phil who found her.

'Finding everything okay?'

She turned in surprise to see him helping himself to a plate of sandwiches, a smile softening his wrinkled face, and she wondered why it had taken her so long to work out the connection. 'Yes, thanks. I'm surprised you got away from the throng surrounding you.'

He chortled. 'It's the quick or the dead in this business. I must say, that boss of yours is a very persuasive man.'

Tegan nodded, reminded of that kiss outside the lift, knowing how close she'd come to being swept completely away. Oh, yes, *she knew how persuasive he could be*. She suppressed a shiver at the memory and dragged her attention back to the business at hand. 'Maverick is passionate about the project, and wanting it to be the best it can be. That's why he wants you on board.'

He shrugged with a nod and took a mouthful of sandwich, and Tegan was once more reminded of Sam. 'You know,' she ventured, 'I hope you don't mind my asking this, but you look so much like someone I know. You're not related to Sam Rogerson, by any chance, are you?'

Phil straightened and his blue eyes sparkled. 'You're a refreshing thing. With that lead up, I was half expecting you to ask me what I thought of Maverick's offer. But yes, my second son is called Sam. He's a doctor with *Médecin Sans Frontières*.'

'I knew it! Sam's a wonderful man and a great doctor, just a natural with the children. The people love it when he visits. You must be very proud of him and the work he's doing.'

'Good God, girl! Don't tell me you've been out to some of those godforsaken places he works in?'

'Oh,' she said, bringing herself up as she remembered who she was supposed to be. Morgan had never been to Africa, let alone anywhere near a refugee camp. 'Actually no, not exactly, but I've heard all about him. My sister was with GlobalAid and got to work closely in the refugee camps with him. She was always telling me how wonderful he is, with the kids especially.'

'Well, you know, that's just so good to hear. Because he's a hopeless correspondent. We might hear from him once or twice a year. Drives Doris and me batty. We never know what he's up to.'

'Then, if it's any consolation, he's doing really well,' she said. 'I know my sister saw him a month ago just before she left the country, and she said he was looking great and loving the work but still missing home and family all the same—especially as it gets closer to Christmas time again.' In fact Sam had been the doctor who'd agreed to her discharge. They'd had a long chat about the Gold Coast and how he envied her going home.

Phil looked at her for a while, shaking his head slowly, his expression contemplative. Then he sighed. 'I don't know what to say. That's wonderful to hear. Just wonderful. And your sister told you all this, you say?'

Tegan threw up a silent prayer for forgiveness. She didn't mean to lie, but what else could she do? 'She just came home after three years away. It all just spilled out. Everything about her life there, and everyone she met. She loved it all.'

'Well, I don't think I have to tell you that you've made my day,' he said. 'Doris will be so happy to hear the news. She worries, you understand, as do I. It's the risk, you see. We don't know what he's going through. And naturally we fear for what might happen to him.'

Tegan nodded, understanding only too well. When she'd come home, Morgan had threatened her life and limb if she ever thought about going away and leaving her again. It was hard on family, she knew. 'Not knowing is the worst,' she agreed. 'But, if it helps at all, I know that the way my sister and a lot of her colleagues rationalise it—they understand there are risks, and do their very best to minimise them, but at the same time they also believe that there are simply times you have to step outside your comfort zone and take a risk if you want to make a difference in this world.'

He seemed to consider her words for a moment before placing one hand on her shoulder and giving it a squeeze. 'Wise words, young lady. Very wise words indeed.' Then he fished a card out from his wallet and handed it to her. 'This has my personal details on it. Call me when your sister's free and we'll arrange a time she can come and talk to us about life in the refugee camps—and what our son's been up to. And thank you again, I can't tell you how thrilled Doris is going to be when I tell her. Now, you better drink your coffee. It'll be getting cold.'

Oh hell, she realised, not her coffee. *Maverick's coffee.* And it was stone cold.

What the blazes was she doing up there? Maverick scowled through the cloud of legalese going on around him and watched. And what the hell could they be talking about that made her smile like that? She'd certainly never flashed a smile like that in his direction.

Then he saw Rogerson reach out an arm and drop it on her shoulder, and his blood pressure spiked. When he saw Rogerson hand her something, his hackles went up twofold.

'Maverick, did you want to add something?'

He looked around to the expectant face of his senior legal counsel, and realised he'd given voice to the growl that had rumbled through him.

'No. Carry on,' he assured them, surprised at the extent of his reaction. It's just the deal, he told himself. If she'd done or had said *anything* that threatened this deal and Rogerson's acceptance of his guarantee then she'd pay. And given the strange mood she'd been in lately...

His coffee appeared before him—*finally*. He looked up to acknowledge its receipt, but her features betrayed no trace of the friendly familiarity he'd seen her sharing with Rogerson just a minute or so ago. Instead it was like she'd pulled down shutters over her face, banishing her smile and removing all trace of interest from those changeable hazel eyes.

Damn!

'Right,' announced Rogerson at the other end of the table. 'I see no point wasting everyone's time any longer. In fact, I think we can safely bring this meeting to a conclusion. Maverick, what say you?'

Maverick's gut roiled as he threw a damning look in his PA's direction. What the hell had she said to him? Whatever it was, she'd pay for it.

He pushed his coffee away untouched. Right now he was unable to drink anything. 'I say,' he managed at last, battling to keep the churning going on inside him out of his voice. 'That all depends on what you have in mind.'

'Well, I've given your proposal some thought, and I've made my decision. I'm not going to accept your personal guarantee.'

CHAPTER FIVE

SOMETHING inside Maverick snapped, cutting his heart-beat short and leaving only one thought in his mind.

Morgan was dead meat.

This project had been years in the making, years in the putting together, and now when they'd been so close it was all falling apart. And she'd said something to Rogerson during that break, something that had made up his mind.

'I see.' The words felt like they'd been ripped from him.

'I'd be surprised if you do,' Phil continued. 'Because the reason I don't want your personal guarantee is because I don't think I need it.'

Maverick's heart tripped back to life with the shock. But that would mean…

'So, you're going to commit to Royalty Cove without the guarantee?'

'Absolutely. Anyone who not only talks like a vision-ary but who is prepared to put their money where their mouth is has to be someone I can put my faith in. Besides, there are some things in life more important than a guaranteed return.' He paused and winked in

Tegan's direction. 'Sometimes it's worth stepping out of one's comfort zone and taking a risk.'

'So what happened back there?' Maverick had been brooding a good ten minutes as he drove from Rogerson's offices.

'What do you mean? You got your deal stitched up, didn't you? At least the Rogerson end of it.'

'That's not what I meant,' he growled, as he swooped around a line of slower vehicles. 'What happened between you and Rogerson? Something was obviously going on—the hand on the shoulder, the wink across the room. What was that all about?'

He took his eyes off the road long enough to see the start of a wry smile. 'Why, Maverick,' she teased. 'Anyone would think you were jealous.'

He flashed her a look that would peel paint, and hoped she'd feel the blowtorch he'd put behind it. Because he could sure feel the glare she was directing his way in return. 'Rogerson's old enough to be your grandfather.'

'So? I liked him. I thought he was genuine and warm, not just another self-aggrandising multi-millionaire out for what he can get.'

Maverick burned. Is that what she thought of him? Is that why she didn't smile at him? But she was wrong. He wasn't jealous—he was livid. 'What did you say to him?'

Out of his peripheral vision he caught her shrug. 'Phil Rogerson has a son called Sam, a doctor working with *Médecin Sans Frontières*.'

'And?'

'And I… And *my sister* worked with him from time to time. We were just talking about that.'

'You have a sister?'

'Just the one.'

'Who works in refugee camps?'

'She works for GlobalAid. Or she did. She just finished up a short time ago.'

'You never told me you had a sister.'

'Maybe you never asked.'

And he never had. He'd never been interested. Not until now. Somehow the topic of Morgan and everything about her—what she did when she went home at night, who she saw—seemed suddenly fascinating.

'So it was your sister who worked with this—what did you call him—Sam Rogerson?'

'That's right.'

'Then how did you know about him?'

Beside him she shifted, and a brief glance revealed she'd turned her attentions out the window.

'She told me.'

'And how did you know Phil was his father?'

She snapped her head around. 'Look, is all this going somewhere?'

He glanced at her, surprised but not entirely disappointed by her outburst. It was much too fascinating. 'You tell me.'

'No, I didn't know, okay? I guessed, and I got lucky. He and his wife hadn't heard from him for a long time, so he was pleased when I told them my sister had seen him just a month ago.'

He steered the car into the underground car park and brought it to a halt, but made no move to exit the car.

'Morgan,' he said when she reached for the handle.

She turned around to face him. 'Yes?'

He slung one arm around the back of her seat and

leant over towards her, not missing that she shrank back towards the door like she was afraid he was going to pounce on her.

Then again, maybe he was.

The idea had appeal, especially if it would be to continue where they'd left off last night. All night he'd thought about that kiss, where it could have gone—where it *would* have gone—if only she hadn't bolted like the hounds of hell were snapping at her heels.

'Did you want something?' she prompted, her hand still on the door handle. Her eyes were suspicious, and her colour was up. Even her breathing was coming too rapid, like she was preparing for battle.

Or something else.

Was she remembering that kiss too? Was she feeling this pull, like it wasn't over, that they still had unfinished business?

'Your sister saw Rogerson's son a month ago. It was remarkable she told you that.'

'Look! What is your problem? I expected you to be happy after that meeting. Didn't you just get what you wanted?'

What he wanted? *What he wanted?* He wasn't sure *what* he wanted lately. Other than right now wanting to kiss his sultry secretary senseless.

But she'd already released the catch and was halfway out.

'Morgan!'

He was out of the car and after her as she made for the lift, her fingers jabbing at the call button like she was clamouring for emergency services.

'Why are you so defensive about this? It *was* nothing short of remarkable,' he said as she stared at the closed lift doors, her chest rising and falling like she'd just run a hundred metres. 'Just as it was nothing short of fortuitous.'

This time she swung her head around, her eyes large and luminous in their surprise. 'Fortuitous?'

She was so sick of his questions, so sick of the constant probing. She knew it was only a matter of time before he caught her out on a lie, a lie that would bring this whole sordid deception tumbling down around her. But he was now saying it was fortuitous. 'I thought you were angry with me.'

'I thought I was too,' he said. 'Because I couldn't work out what you'd done to bring Rogerson around.'

She shook her head, but whether it was to argue with his words, or more as a protest against his menacing proximity, she wasn't sure. He was too close, like a dark presence bearing down upon her, focusing on her so intently it was difficult to breathe. Difficult to think.

It had been easier when he'd been antagonistic, easier when he'd been distant, and a dark fury like a storm cloud had hung over him.

The lift arrived and she fled into the relative sanctuary. A sanctuary that became a prison cell when she turned and realised she was now trapped in a metal box with the very man from whom she'd been trying to escape.

He inserted a card key and pushed a button that would take them uninterrupted to his penthouse office, but then, instead of staying by her side like she was hoping, he turned so his back was to the doors. She flattened herself hard against the wall of the lift, feeling the hand rail pressing into the small of her back.

'Don't you see,' he said, moving even closer, planting a hand on the wall beside her head when the lift jerked into motion, 'that if your sister hadn't told you that she'd seen Sam, and if you hadn't thought to mention it today, then Rogerson's response might have been a very different one? He went into this meeting shaky about committing, but something you said made the difference. What did you tell him?'

He was too close. Way too close, so she could feel his heat curling into hers; way too close, so she could study the individual whiskers that made a shadow in the cleft of his chin. And if she could feel his scent wrap around her like a silken ribbon and tug her even closer then he was so close it was damn near fatal. She battled for control of her tongue, felt even that shred of control slipping dangerously away.

'I don't know,' she managed at last. 'Phil was saying he worried about his son taking risks in difficult circumstances, and I just told him that sometimes it's worthwhile taking risks if you want to make a difference.'

His eyes glinted in the light and the corners of his mouth turned up. 'Oh, bravo,' he uttered, a low rumbling whisper that turned her scattered thoughts and her bones to jelly. 'I gave a long speech about what the project meant for the world and our respective businesses. But somehow you managed to encapsulate what the project meant on a personal basis, for the one man who could've put paid to the entire agreement. But who didn't.'

He reached his free hand out and she flinched, pushing herself back even farther against the cold half-mirrored wall behind her, the hand rail pressing deeper into her spine. But his touch was gentle, little more than mere fingertips against the line of her cheek and jaw.

So why was it enough to set her flesh aflame? Why did it set her breasts to aching—*yearning*—fullness?

Her teeth grappled with her bottom lip. The last time they'd been so close it had ended badly. But then she'd imagined he was interested in Morgan. Her sister had soon put paid to that. Which could only mean that for whatever crazy, nonsensical reason he was interested in her—*Tegan*!

And how was she supposed to fight that?

But then, why *should* she?

Because Morgan is coming back, a tiny remaining shred of sanity in Tegan's head insisted. *And it's Morgan who'll have to live with any consequences.*

'Maverick…' she pleaded.

He tilted his head, his eyes firmly focused on her mouth. 'I should thank you,' he muttered. 'You saved the deal. I should find some way to repay you.'

'There's no need,' she said too quickly, looking to the side, thinking she could just slip along the back wall of the lift and get some breathing space.

His free hand landed in front of her face, cutting off her escape, imprisoning her in the cage of his arms and drawing her closer with the vacuum of his heat. 'I could at the very least say thank you.'

She turned to look at him, and immediately wished she hadn't. Brooding magnetism and 'angel of doom' qualities stared back at her. *And she knew she was doomed.*

'So say it,' she whispered breathlessly, recognising a stab of disappointment that all this build-up could lead to nothing more than a gravelly thank you, but wanting nothing more than to end this loaded anticipation if it was to lead nowhere. Logically there was nowhere for it to go.

He lifted one hand from the wall to curl one finger under her chin, angling her head higher. 'But mere thanks hardly seems enough for what you've done.'

Blood rushed loud in her ears, a sensual thumping that slowed her thoughts and reactions, and threatened to swamp logic entirely.

And meanwhile the lift slid inexorably skywards, up to where the air was thinner. Already she was feeling the effects—the dizziness, the congealed thought processes. *It had to be the altitude.*

'Then…' she ventured uncertainly, wishing for an end to the suspense—to the anticipation. 'Then, what?'

His face was like a mask, all stillness, its harsh angles and planes held together by a dark, brooding magnetism that screamed control but looked set to snap. Only his eyes betrayed the turmoil going on inside— dark and filled with heat and burning with desire— desire for *her*. It was all she could do not to launch herself into their molten depths.

He dropped his elbows to the lift wall, framing her face with his forearms, his face hovering just above hers, his warm breath mingling with hers. Her breasts pressed into his chest, the slightest movement setting up a delicious friction that charged them to an aching tautness, turning her already tight nipples bullet-hard.

'Then…*this.*'

His lips met hers—not so much a kiss as a caress. She melted into him on a sigh. A sigh of relief. A sigh of homecoming.

And it was exactly like coming home. It was like finding your way back to somewhere special and knowing you never wanted to leave again.

If he'd been rougher, if he'd been forceful, she might have found cause to resist—but as it was he moved his mouth so gently; so warmly did he share this meeting of lips that there was nothing to endure, nothing to resist. Only to welcome. His tongue traced the line of her teeth, invited hers into the dance, and she trembled into his mouth. Instinctively she reached out her hands, needing to find purchase on something solid lest her knees give way and her legs buckle beneath her.

A pinging noise brought her back to reality, reminding her of where they were. With a cushioned bump the lift came to a halt and the doors hissed open. He lifted his mouth a fraction, his forehead resting on hers, his breath ragged. 'Oh my God,' he rasped, and Tegan knew without doubt that he was experiencing the same overwhelming sensations as she.

Then in one deft movement he scooped her up into his arms and, without saying a word, carried her from the lift. She gasped, at once shocked and yet grateful, certain she would never have managed to exit the lift on her shaky legs. The sheer thrill of being swept up into his strong arms—her body cradled next to his, the thump of his heartbeat reverberating through her body—was intoxicatingly heady. So heady that she barely registered that he'd failed to stop to let her down next to her work station. He didn't stop at the anteroom beyond, and when he swept her purposefully through his own office she began to have an uncomfortable sense that maybe today Maverick intended on finishing up what he'd been denied before.

He looked resolutely ahead, the set of his jaw firm, his expression grim, and a thread of panic wound through her and yanked tight.

'Where are you taking me?'

'Somewhere private, where we won't be disturbed.' Without letting go of her, he turned a door handle, kicking open the door in front of them.

'Maverick!' she protested, squirming in arms that held her like prison bonds close to him. 'I don't think this is such a good idea.'

'Right now, I can't think of a better one.'

He had a point. But, while her body applauded his initiative, a part of her registered the core truth. It still didn't make it a good idea. This could *never* be a good idea.

He marched her through a large sitting-room that, like his office, overlooked the glorious stretch of beach that made up the long golden sweep of the Gold Coast. But this was hardly the time to appreciate the vista, not when he was heading still deeper into his private suite.

'Put me down. This is a mistake!'

'There's no mistake,' he replied, his voice sounding strained and dangerous. 'But I'll put you down, seeing you ask so nicely.'

It wasn't the easy setting-down on the floor she'd been anticipating. With a strangled cry she felt herself launched through the air, landing with a thud in the middle of the wide, silken-covered monster of a bed, and she only just caught his jacket being tossed lazily in the other direction.

He placed one knee on the bed and looked down at her, his eyes like dark fire, his hands at his shirt cuffs popping his buttons free before starting on his shirt front, working his way down, button by button.

'Oh, no,' she said, scurrying for the edge of the bed, even as a thrill of arousal shimmied through her blood.

She had to get out of here. So why did her muscles feel so unresponsive? Why was she so loath to leave this bed? And why did such a delicious heat curl warm and damp between her thighs?

He reefed out his shirt from his pants and hauled it off. This time her gasp was one of appreciation. He was simply beautiful, his chest and shoulders every bit as magnificent as they'd felt, his sculpted torso an artist's delight. *And every woman's.*

'You felt it back there,' he whispered, not letting go of the laser-like hold on her eyes. 'You felt what was happening between us in that lift.'

'It was just a kiss,' she pleaded, knowing she was lying, knowing he knew it.

'It was more than just a kiss,' he argued, dropping his hands to his waist.

Oh God!

There was no air in the room, no oxygen, and no hope for her unless she did something soon. She forced herself to the side of the bed farthest away, pushing herself up on shaky legs.

'But that doesn't mean…'

He rounded the bed to cut her off. He took one of her trembling hands and pressed it to his lips. 'It means you want me.' He hesitated a fraction as he stared down at her, before taking her hand and moving it lower until her fingers cupped his length. Breath dragged through his teeth as her fingers found purchase. He was so big, so hard, the power evident. Power waiting to be unleashed within her.

'And, God knows,' he hissed, as she couldn't help but test his firmness with her hand, 'I want you.'

His mouth descended to hers once more as he crushed her to him, and she shuddered into the truth of his all-powerful embrace.

And it felt so right. It was so welcoming; so welcome and so right.

But even as his hands stirred her body, sweeping up and down in a sensual dance of persuasion, tears of futility squeezed from her eyes.

Another time, in other circumstances, and things would have been different; she could have acted to satisfy this desperate yearning, this desperate need which saw her abandoning everything she'd ever thought of love or romance. It was insane; she'd known this man just two days and here she was so close to giving herself up to him. She wanted to give herself up to him. But it was too quick, it was too passionate, and it was too all-consuming.

It was madness.

A madness she couldn't give in to—not now, not with Maverick. Not when she was supposed to be someone else, and that someone else would be returning to this job, never expecting the mess Tegan would have been leaving for her.

'I can't do this,' she pleaded.

'But you want this,' he soothed, his tongue laving her throat, stirring her senses like nothing she'd ever known before. 'You want me inside you.'

Yes! she wanted to scream, shocked at her own wantonness but still coherent enough to know that if she admitted anything she was lost.

'No,' she lied, searching for new stocks of resolve just as quickly as it flowed out of her. 'I don't want you. I want you to stop.'

He stilled on a long exhale without letting go of her, the tension in his bunched muscles like a caged lion clawing to be set free. 'You really mean that?' Then he lifted his head and stared at her, the heat in his eyes giving way to surprise. He touched fingertips to her cheek. 'You're not crying?'

She took advantage of his concern and wheeled away, swiping at her face with one hand. 'I have to go.'

He moved to bridge the gap, and she moved still farther away, closer to the door that would take her from this room, take her from Maverick—*remove her from temptation.*

'Morgan,' he urged. 'What's wrong?'

Me! she wanted to scream. *I'm what's wrong, can't you see that?* But instead she said, 'I don't want to make love with you. Don't you understand? Just like you really don't want me.'

'What are you talking about?' he protested. 'That's not true. I do want you. You know that.'

She shook her head. Morgan had told her exactly how things were between her and her boss, and Tegan knew exactly how Morgan would expect things to be when she came back Monday morning. The last thing she would be expecting would be her boss wanting to carry her off into his den at the drop of a hat.

'It is true!' she flung at him, her chest heaving, her defences at breaking point—because if this didn't work she would be lost. 'What was the line you used when I started work here? *"I don't do PAs."* Isn't that what you said from the very beginning? So what the hell do you think you're trying to prove now?'

White-hot fury devoured him like a lava flow. Yes, he'd told her that—maybe not as crassly as the words she'd employed, but he'd made his position clear.

But it was *his* line. It had been *his* decision. And to have it thrown back at him by her…

'Go home,' he said once the rush of blood in his ears had finally settled down to a dull roar. 'Take the afternoon off.'

'I have work to do—'

'Go home!' he repeated, louder this time. 'You've already done enough.'

More than enough, if it all came down to it. And she'd reminded him of too much in the process, of a woman who'd wanted everything and had left him with nothing, and of a vow he'd made never to let that happen again.

He picked up his shirt from the floor, shrugged it on and did up his buttons with a hell of a lot less satisfaction than he'd undone them a few minutes before.

Damn that vow. But he'd had good reason back then to make a vow like that. He'd had good reason to make it clear to anyone who worked that closely with him that they shouldn't get ideas.

Which hadn't stopped him getting ideas.

What was happening to him? Morgan had worked for him for eighteen months and he'd never so much as looked at her, and now suddenly it was like he'd taken the blinkers off and discovered the woman who hid behind her 'repel all boarders' outfits.

And he wanted her.

And why shouldn't he have her? She was nothing like Tina. If she had been, she would hardly have put up with him without making a move for the time she'd been with him. She would have been off to secure another, more receptive mark. And even now she wasn't racing to fall into his bed. She wanted him, he could tell, but she was fighting it.

Which made her all the more refreshingly attractive.

So why was she holding back? It wasn't like they didn't know each other. So what that in the past he'd barely got past 'Good morning' and 'Type this up' on the conversation scale, it wasn't like they were strangers. So what was her problem? Why should she drag up something he'd said so long ago and use it against him?

He tucked in his shirt and raked his fingers through his hair, feeling a familiar tension curling inside him. He needed a woman, and there was more than one way to skin a cat.

He strode into his office, picked up his PDA and threw himself into his chair. He had a list of phone numbers as long as his arm. He'd find someone more accommodating with no trouble.

He scrolled through the numbers, finally coming to a halt when he found one that halfway appealed. Sonya—all short, sleek black hair and greyhound leanness—she'd do fine. And she'd never been able to say no to him. He was halfway through dialling when he slammed the phone down in disgust.

He didn't want Sonya. Not when he had a different face taunting him, a different body telling him she didn't want him, turning him down flat.

And all because of something that had happened years ago.

Damn it! Tina was still finding a way to ruin his life. That damned promise he'd made because of her was coming back to haunt him. As far as he was concerned, it was his vow and nobody else's. It was up to him if he damn well broke it.

And Morgan had just better get used to the idea.

She'd come around. He'd give her to the end of the week. All he had to do was wait…

CHAPTER SIX

WEDNESDAY dawned bright and sunny all along the Gold Coast—unless you happened to be in Tegan's head. If only she'd insisted on Morgan coming home when she'd called Monday night, and had not let herself be talked out of it, this charade would be over now. Instead she had another three days of Maverick to endure, another three days of trying to ignore his heated presence, another three days of fighting this inconvenient attraction.

And as the day wore on she waited for him to make another move on her. But it didn't come.

Instead all Wednesday he hovered like a dark angel, brooding and intense, finding any excuse to leave his office to ask her a question or to drop something on her desk, and watching over everything she did. Watching her until she wanted to scream with the tension.

Five p.m. had never looked so good. She practically fled from the office, but she'd survived.

Thursday his mood was blacker, his efforts redoubled. When he emerged from his office, for what had to have been the third time in the space of ten minutes, she felt like throwing her hands up and screaming, *'Enough!'*

'What is it *this* time?' she asked instead, unable to keep the aggravation from her voice.

But instead of rummaging through her files, searching for some mysterious document before slamming the cabinet shut and marching off discontentedly as he'd done so many times previously, he surprised her by dropping some pages on her desk. 'Rogerson needs this chart, but we both want some changes made first. Get on to someone in Projects and have them get this back to me on the double.'

He turned as Tegan looked at the project-development chart and Maverick's handwritten notes and wondered what the drama was. She'd cut her teeth doing such tasks in her previous office job before she'd felt the need to do something more hands on and had joined GlobalAid. 'There's no need. I can do this for you right away.'

He looked back at her. 'Since when have you used project-development software?'

She blinked. 'Since I did a course. At night. Didn't I mention it?'

His eyes narrowed. 'All right,' he said, his voice heavy with doubt. 'Get Projects to send you the file. Then I want it on my desk in ten minutes.'

She had it there in seven.

Not that it improved Maverick's disposition. That and the fact she'd done it all perfectly only seemed to further foul his mood. 'Well, well, well,' he muttered, regarding her steadily over the pages of the chart. 'You appear to have many hidden talents. I wonder what other surprises you have in store for me?'

She swallowed under his leaden scrutiny and made a mental note to enrol Morgan on the next available project-development course.

'If that's all, then…' she suggested, just wanting to escape.

'No, it's not all,' he barked, launching himself from his chair and rounding the desk towards her.

She took a step backwards. It had been two days since he'd tried anything. Two days of praying he wouldn't touch her, knowing she couldn't trust herself if he did. *Two days of secretly wishing he would.*

He came to a halt in front of her, his wide shoulders blocking out the vista, his gunslinger dark looks becoming the view, and she trembled in anticipation.

His eyes scoured her face, settling on her mouth. His own lips looked like an invitation, parting slightly as she waited.

Then he offered her the papers she hadn't realised he was still holding. 'Fax this to Rogerson right away.'

On Friday she was over her momentary weakness. Friday had never felt better. It didn't matter that Maverick had been in the worst mood he'd been in all week, a bad mood that seemed to have gotten progressively darker by the minute, because in just sixty short minutes she'd be out of here, out of the office for ever and away from Maverick. No more brooding tension; no more putting up with long, loaded looks; no more repressing urges that longed to be satisfied.

And Tegan couldn't wait.

She'd made it. She'd lasted an entire week with Maverick without him suspecting a thing. Morgan's job was safe, and any and all debts she owed her sister were now well and truly paid in full.

She was humming to herself when Maverick emerged from his office, a stack of paperwork in his hands. 'What are you so happy about?'

She looked up at his scowling face, and once again felt that jolt that hit her every time she looked at him. She also felt something like a stab of disappointment. Life would be a lot simpler from now on but she was going to miss the electricity. Likewise, she'd miss the sparring and the heat. But those things didn't stop her smiling now, not when she was so close to achieving her goal.

'It's Friday.'

Maverick's scowl deepened. 'And?'

Like she was going to explain it? She shrugged, belying the sheer intoxication of it all. Success fizzed like champagne in her veins. 'Everyone loves Fridays.' *Especially me,* she thought, *especially today.*

'You have plans?'

Just picking up my sister tomorrow from the airport and reclaiming my life! She couldn't help but smile up at him, despite his scowl. Or maybe because of it. 'Just the usual,' she said.

He made a sound like a snarl and headed back to his office.

Maverick had never seen her smile so much. He threw himself into his chair and regarded his desk solemnly. Instead of warming to him like he'd planned, in the last few days she'd kept her distance, keeping any and all contact with him to a minimum, her hazel eyes chilled to ice chips. For days she'd never sent so much as a smile his way. Now her face was lit up brighter than a Christmas tree.

And he had the uncomfortable feeling she wasn't smiling with him—she was smiling *at* him.

And he didn't like it one bit.

His computer registered incoming email. Halfheartedly he glanced over, sitting up in his chair when he recognised the sender. He opened the mail and read.

'Yes!' he yelled, slamming his fist onto the desk before picking up his phone and dialling.

She'd closed down her computer and cleaned up the desk. Her glance moved over a wad of papers sitting in the filing tray and Tegan smiled to herself. *Welcome home, Morgan.*

She pulled her handbag strap over her shoulder and sighed, a long, cathartic 'glad to be done' sigh. It was over. All that remained was to say goodnight to Maverick and she'd be gone. She'd never have to see him again. She'd never have to put up with his dark gun-slinger good looks or hot and heavy glances. She'd never more have to endure his heated magnetism.

She'd never have to endure another kiss.

Something squeezed down tight inside her. Who was she trying to kid? His kisses had never been something to endure. Instead they'd been like an awakening. And now, for ever, she'd be left wondering how it might have been if things had been different and she'd been in a position where she didn't have to reject his advances, where she could have allowed Maverick to awaken every last part of her.

Now she'd never know.

She took a deep breath. It was for the best. She knew that. Taking care of her sister's job for the week had never included taking care of her boss.

It was time to go. She headed through the anteroom to say goodnight and slammed into a wall coming out.

'Morgan!' She felt his big hands steady her momentarily, before feeling herself lifted from the ground and spun around in his arms. He set her back down without letting go of her, leaving her breathless and dizzy, and looked down, his dark eyes glinting, his mouth curved into a wicked smile. 'Giuseppe Zeppa's regained consciousness and demanding to know why the deal hasn't been stitched up. He's giving them hell over there.'

She couldn't help but smile back at him, knowing what it meant to him, his excitement infectious. 'That's great. I'm really pleased.'

'And I've just been on the phone to Rogerson, who can't wait to get started.'

His eyes crinkled and he looked her over, taking in her bag at her shoulder. 'What are you doing?'

'I'm going home. I was just coming to say goodnight.'

'Not now, you're not. This calls for a celebration. We're going out for dinner.'

She tried to take a step back, but he still had hold of her arms. 'Maverick, I don't think—'

'Rogerson's expecting you to be there. I promised him you'd come along.'

'You had no right!'

'Why? You said you had nothing special happening. What have you got to lose?'

Just my resolve. She looked down at her clothes. 'I can't go out like this, I'm not dressed for dinner.'

'It's still early. I'll drive you home and you can get changed.'

Her arms tingled where he held her; every part of her seemed to hum with his proximity, and temptation hung thick on the air. She'd almost escaped. She'd almost been home free, and now she was facing one last evening with him.

But why did the thought of that thrill her more than

it should? It was a business dinner—admittedly a celebration, but with Phil Rogerson and the legal and financial teams there what could possibly happen? And yet still she felt a bubble of glee that her time with Maverick need not come to an end just yet.

'Okay,' she agreed on an impulse she hoped she didn't live to regret. 'Seeing Phil asked me too, I'll come.'

Maverick was waiting outside the car taking a call when she emerged nervously from the townhouse. She saw him glance up at her and still before snapping shut his phone and standing to attention, the look in his eyes one of unadulterated appreciation.

'You look fantastic,' he said, swinging open the passenger door for her and suddenly she halted as warmth bloomed inside her. She felt afraid again, afraid of what might happen, afraid of what she couldn't deny.

'What is it?' he pressed. 'What's wrong?'

'I'm just not convinced this is such a good idea.'

His eyes revealed nothing of the frustration he had to be feeling right now. He tilted his head indulgently at her. 'Rogerson felt the same way this week. He wasn't sure whether he should commit to the deal. But you convinced him that sometimes it's worth taking that risk. Maybe you should take a spoonful of your own medicine?'

She shivered. It wasn't the same, she wanted to argue. Rogerson stood to gain by taking a risk on Maverick. Whereas she… She stood to lose everything—Morgan's job, her own sanity and, most of all, she feared, her heart.

Was it a risk she could so easily brush off?

No.

Was it a risk she was willing to take?

Oh, yes.

She shivered as she slipped past him and lowered herself into the car, his eyes doing crazy things to her blood and her breasts at the same time.

Business dinner, she persisted in telling herself, *it's still only a business dinner*. But that hadn't stopped her finding the most feminine dress she could find in her sister's wardrobe, a soft floral pastel with crossover bodice and pleated waist that gave way to a floaty skirt that shifted when she moved, revealing glimpses of leg. After the dull business suits she'd been wearing all week, this dress felt soft, feminine—and, the way it felt against her skin, even a little sexy.

The way he looked at her made it even more so.

He climbed in alongside but didn't drive away. Instead he just looked across at her. 'I've never seen you with your hair down,' he said, touching a hand to the waves that cascaded around her face and over her shoulders, twisting one tendril around his finger, a gentle pressure that had her whole scalp tingling. 'I like it.'

Their eyes connected and for the space of one hitched breath the world stopped. She drank him in with her eyes, the early-evening light turning his features into a play of light and shadow, of dark depths and rich promise, and she realised that just one evening with this man would never be enough.

She forced her eyes away as a stab of regret lanced her heart. *Because one last night was all she had.*

With a sigh he let go and started the engine. 'Do you mind if we make a brief detour on the way? I've just had a call and there's someone I need to drop in on.'

She shrugged. 'Sure,' she said, already enjoying the

scent of fine leather and an even finer driver, and not in any particular rush to put an end to the sensual pleasure.

It was only when he pulled into the gated car park of the Green Valley Rest Home that her curiosity was piqued.

She looked up at him, her question unspoken.

'My grandmother,' he simply said.

'You have a grandmother?'

He flashed a look at her. 'That surprises you?'

'Yes. I mean no. I mean…' What did she mean—that it seemed incongruous for a man as hard as Maverick to have family, let alone a little old grandmother?

'Besides,' he continued, a slight frown creasing his brow as he parked the car and pulled on the handbrake, 'you knew about Nell—given you're the one who sends her flowers for her every birthday and Mother's Day.'

'Oh, of course, *that* grandmother,' she stumbled, feeling her cheeks burn and wishing she were some place else entirely. 'But you send them, I just order them.'

He was already climbing out, and thankfully oblivious to her gaffe. 'I'll be as quick as I possibly can.'

But he wasn't out the door before a wiry old woman on a walking frame came through the front doors.

'Jimmy!' she snapped out in a soft American drawl. 'What took you so long?'

Maverick didn't flinch at his grandmother's use of his childhood name. He just leant down and kissed her sunken cheek. 'Come on, Nell,' he said, taking her by one arm. 'You should be inside now. It's getting late.'

'It's only late if you're on nursing-home hours!' she grumbled, pulling her arm out of his hand. 'I swear it's a conspiracy to get us to sleep twelve hours of the day.'

'Okay,' he conceded, motioning to a park bench nearby. 'Let's sit outside and you can tell me what's so important that you had to see me straight away.'

He waited while she negotiated the few short steps to the bench and got into position, lowering herself down slowly behind her frame, before he sat down alongside her.

'So what's the problem, Gran?'

'Christmas.'

She spat the word out like a bullet. He sighed. This was the emergency the staff had called him around to deal with? But still he sympathised. When Nell got something stuck in her head, there was no way to put her off the track.

'Christmas is over six weeks away, Nell.'

'I know that. But what are you doing about it?'

He hadn't given it a thought. They'd probably do the same as they'd done in previous years—he'd book a lunch somewhere, and if she was bright enough on the day they'd eat out together, or otherwise he'd spend a large chunk of the day just sitting with her at the home and taking her to enjoy an ice cream at the beach.

'What would you like me to do about it?'

'Well, you might do something about getting the whole family together for a change. If you don't do something soon, Frank and Sylvia are bound to be booked up again.'

He pressed his lips together and nodded stoically, burying his own feelings. There was no point telling her while she was in this state that her son and daughter-in-law had been permanently booked up for five years now. Instead he hooked an arm around her bony shoulders and gave her a gentle squeeze. 'I'll see what I can do, okay?'

'And who's the girl in the car?'

He groaned to himself. There was nothing wrong with his grandmother's eyesight, that was for sure.

'It's just Morgan, my PA.'

'Funny name for a girl.' She chewed on her bottom lip while she peered through wrinkle-rimmed eyes at the car. 'So she's the one who sends me all those flowers, then?'

'Those flowers are actually from me.'

'Rubbish. I bet you never bought flowers in your life. I suppose I should thank her in that case.'

'There's no need—'

She hauled herself up behind her Zimmer frame and regarded him sharply. 'Why? You're not ashamed of your own flesh and blood, are you?'

'No, of course not.'

'Then what's stopping you?' she demanded, waving him away with a flick of her wizened wrist.

He was almost at the car when he met Tegan getting out, her dress waving softly in the breeze, the wave in her hair flicking like it was alive. He smiled apologetically. 'She wants to meet you.'

'I gathered that.'

'Don't let her get to you,' he warned her softly. 'She can be a bit sharp.'

'Yoo-hoo,' called the old woman from behind them. 'I'm waiting.'

Tegan smiled and let herself be led the short distance and introduced to his grandmother.

'It's a pleasure to meet you, Mrs Maverick.'

'Oh, my dear,' said the old woman, taking one of her hands in her own. Skin like crêpe paper betrayed her age, but there was a strength to the old woman's grip, and an inner heat that resonated through her. 'You simply must call me Nell.' Then she frowned. 'Though I must say you don't look much like a Morgan to me. Are you sure that's your name?'

'Gran—' interrupted Maverick.

'Much too pretty for a Morgan,' she continued, undaunted. 'Yes,' she said, with a final jerk of Tegan's hands. 'I think I shall call you Vanessa.'

Tegan laughed nervously while doing her best to avoid Maverick's eyes. 'That's fine, Nell.'

'Now,' she said, easing herself down onto the bench once more and pulling Tegan down alongside her in the process. 'Did I ever tell you about the time I got lost in the mountains as a little girl and almost got eaten by a bear? No, I don't think I did.' She patted the younger woman on the hand while Maverick stood by and rolled his eyes. 'Well, I was only a tiny tot at the time, four or five at the most…'

'Your gran's a real character.'

They were heading towards the restaurant, having driven most of the way in companionable silence, Tegan content to enjoy the colours of the city lighting as evening passed into night, and to think about this new side to Maverick. He'd been different with Nell, softer and more caring than she'd ever have imagined him to be. The caring grandson—it was as far from ruthless businessman as you could probably get, and totally unexpected. Up until now she'd believed he only cared about his beloved Royalty Cove and in getting what he wanted. But he obviously loved his grandmother deeply. 'I really like her.'

'I got the impression the feeling was mutual.' He

looked over at her with warm-chocolate eyes that made her melt into the upholstery. *Sizzle factor*, that was what he had. Even when they were ostensibly talking about his grandmother, he could still melt her bones with just one glance.

'Thank you,' he said.

She blinked, confused. 'For what?'

'For handling her so well. She's not always easy to deal with. You seemed to cheer her up a lot.'

She smiled. 'I really enjoyed hearing those stories about growing up on the ranch back in Montana.'

He grunted. 'Then you obviously haven't heard them anywhere near enough.'

She laughed out loud. 'So what was it that brought your family to Australia?'

'Oh, the usual I guess. My father fell in love with a girl backpacking through the US. He followed her here to Queensland to convince her to go home with him, when he saw some real opportunities Down Under and gave up on convincing her and instead started convincing Nell to join them out here. They did well. Back in the eighties he was behind a lot of the development of the Gold Coast.'

'Where are they now?'

'Dead. Five years ago, in a light-plane crash. Nell has trouble remembering sometimes.'

Mentally she kicked herself. She should have seen that coming, given Nell's comment about a certain Frank and Sylvia not making it to Christmas. His parents, obviously. 'I'm so sorry. I didn't realise. I know what it's like to lose a parent. But I can't imagine what it must be like to lose a child. That must be so hard for her.' Instinctively she reached out a hand to his arm and squeezed. 'I guess it's probably something I'd rather forget too, if I were in her position. It's lucky she's got you.'

Was it? He'd never thought so. But right now he had more important things on his mind. He looked down at her hand, liking the way her long fingers and tapered nails looked on his arm, liking the way it felt, liking even more what it meant.

Tonight she seemed different. More receptive. Less defensive. And for once she wasn't running. She was touching him. Of her own free will. And the low explosion that had hit him in the gut and burst into flame when he'd seen her emerge tonight in that floaty number fired up again on all burners.

He pulled up at a red light, caught her hand in his and lifted it, pressing her palm against her mouth. He felt the shudder move through her. He caught her gasp and the sharp rise of her chest. And still she didn't pull away.

He gave her hand a final squeeze before setting it back in her lap as the lights turned green.

Tonight,' he said. 'Tonight I think it's me who's the lucky one.'

CHAPTER SEVEN

SHE was intoxicated before she entered the restaurant, intoxicated before she had even one sip of the glass of fine champagne Phil Rogerson pressed into her hands, already giddy with one heated car ride with a man named Maverick.

A meal was ordered and consumed, and somehow she managed to eat enough to convince everyone she was fine before her plate disappeared. A band played softly in the background but the music made no sense in her head. Conversation went on around her, fast paced and celebratory, and at times she even participated—how, she didn't know. Because her mind was fully focused on only one man here tonight, her body one hundred per cent focused on what his loaded gaze was doing to her libido.

It was like someone had turned a switch inside her that said it was okay to feel these things, it was okay to feel this way. *It was okay to want him.*

Then the meal was over and Phil Rogerson and others from his team had drifted away, back to families and their homes. When Maverick simply said, 'Dance with me,' she knew in her heart it was the point of no return.

One last night, she thought, not wanting it to end just yet, *one last opportunity...*

She took his hand and stood, and looked into dark eyes that were asking much, much more of her.

'Yes,' she simply told him, and let him lead her to the dance floor. The music was soft and romantic and made for lovers, and it was no chore to pretend, no chore to melt into his warm embrace and feel herself become part of the music, part of him.

Her head rested against his shoulder, his solid heartbeat beating out a rhythm that beckoned to her, his arms surrounding her and holding her to him like a prize.

Yes, she thought as her body moved with his in a sensual play of flesh against fabric against flesh, a delicious friction that curled deep down inside and pooled heavy and insistent between her thighs.

Yes, her mind screamed when he dipped his head and breathed hot desire into her ear, and made all things possible.

One night would work. Just one night. It happened all the time, after all, especially when there was champagne involved. And Maverick would be satisfied— once would be enough to end this crazy pursuit, and he'd no doubt be happy to forget the whole sordid affair by then. Which would take the heat off Morgan when she returned to work.

It could work. She'd make it work.

The number had finished, but Maverick seemed as reluctant as she was to let go.

'Would you like to keep dancing?' he whispered.

She prised her head from his chest then, and stared into his dark, aching eyes. 'The dancing is nice,' she admitted, her heart banging loud in her chest. 'But I'd rather make love with you.'

A moment. A slow blink. She saw the kick in his throat when he swallowed as her words registered, she felt the thud of his heart, and she felt the corresponding thump of her own when his glinting eyes transmitted their approval.

'Let's go,' he croaked.

They were barely outside when he kissed her the first time, spinning her against the wall, pinning her there while his mouth spun magic upon hers.

I must be drunk, she thought, wanting to laugh with exhilaration, wanting to cry with madness, wanting to melt away into the darkness and have him now.

Somehow they made it to the car, and eventually, with a groan of desperation, he once again tore his mouth from hers long enough to get the car into motion.

She sat side-on, tracing her fingers down his shadowed jaw, for once able to indulge her wants and urges, eager to learn all she could about how this man felt under her hands.

He snared her fingers and dragged her hand to his mouth, planting a kiss on the palm of her hand that was so hot it threatened to melt her bones.

He looked across at her, a gaze so filled with barely controlled longing that it took her breath away. 'Do you have any idea how much I want you right now?' he asked.

She didn't doubt it. One look at the tight planes of his face, the flare of his nostrils, was evidence enough of the control he was forced to exercise in waiting. But still she was tempted. She ran her hand up one leg, rounding his thigh and finding his long, hard length straining for release.

Breath hissed through his teeth.

'I want you too,' she whispered, her voice husky, the reality of what they were about to do setting her body to preparedness, softening her tissues in anticipation.

He stilled her hand. 'Two minutes,' he said through gritted teeth. 'Just two minutes.'

He pulled off the highway and through a gated estate, finally crossing a bridge to a tiny island. He hit a button on a remote control and the gate slid away, revealing a verdant driveway leading to a low-line house set amongst the palms that looked like it was made of almost nothing but glass.

'Welcome to my home,' he said, pulling up alongside, rounding the car to open her door. 'For when I manage to get away from the office.'

'Oh wow,' she said, taking in the moonlight glinting off the water. 'An island paradise built for one.'

He curled an arm around her neck and reeled her in. 'And, tonight, an island paradise built for two.'

She shuddered as he collected her in his arms and brought his mouth to hers. This time there was no need to limit the kiss; now there was no reason to end it. In an instant she was back on that steep ascent, being taken higher and yet higher, his chest crushing her breasts, one leg insinuated between her own, the sleek lines of his car holding her upright.

His hands rounded her, sculpting her like she was clay and he was the master craftsman, his hands setting her skin alight. His mouth laved at her throat, as impatiently he nuzzled aside her shoulder strap. One side of her bodice slipped away, then the other, and he took full advantage, peeling the fabric down, cupping her lace-covered breast with his hands before dispensing even with that.

Exposed in the balmy night air, she arched her back involuntarily, thrusting her breasts farther into his hands, grinding her hips against his hardness. She was a mess of pulsing nerve endings, a mess of need. And there was only one way to ease this interminable ache.

'Maverick!' she cried, and he seemed to sense her distress.

'I know,' he growled, scooping up handfuls of her skirt and tracing up her legs. His eyes sparked when he encountered the lace tops of her stockings.

'Oh God, I was hoping you were wearing these,' he said, moving his hands to cup her behind. He pressed her to him momentarily, and she felt the full effect of his power against her belly. Then she gasped as he lifted her, sliding her fractionally onto the sleek hood of the car, before sliding one hand between her thighs and touching her there where her need was greatest.

She gave a strangled cry, and his last shred of control seemed to evaporate. He shrugged down her pants with one hand like the last act of a desperate man, exposing her to the kiss of the gentle breeze while he freed himself with the other hand.

She guided him to her, even as he battled to don protection, and she felt that jolt of first, come-in-spinner contact, and the tingling invitation of her muscles welcoming him home. She didn't have long to wait. He powered into her on one long thrust that took both their breaths away. They stayed locked that way together for what seemed like long seconds, savouring the feel of each other, before he slowly withdrew, a painful goodbye, then blessedly pressed himself home again in another long thrust, and then another.

She wrapped her legs around him and gave herself

up to the sensations, lost herself in a rhythm powered by a far greater primal beat, lost herself in him.

The night air caressed them even as the fire burned between them, even as the flames burned brighter and more urgent.

Even as the blaze consumed her in one long, shuddering explosion.

She clung to him, weak and spent, her breathing jagged, suddenly feeling exposed and self-conscious in her half nakedness.

'Maybe now,' he whispered between breaths as he drew the straps of her dress up to cover her breasts, 'we might make it as far as the house.'

She chuckled, silently thanking him for defusing the moment, and felt him lift her chin. He looked down at her with a look so deep she shuddered to the core. 'Do you have any idea what your smile does to me?'

Warmth rolled over her in a heated wave. Oh Lord, but he shouldn't say things like that to her. He shouldn't give her ideas. Tonight was about lust, about scratching an itch, and he shouldn't go putting thoughts in her head, thoughts of what could never be.

He pressed his lips to hers as he swung her into his arms and strode purposefully with her to the house, through rooms, until he set her down in the centre of an enormous bed. Full-length windows brought the garden and swaying palms indoors, their shifting fronds dancing in the dappled moonlight.

'Now,' he said. 'Where were we?' He shrugged off his jacket and undid his shirt, and Tegan was reminded of another time, another place, when he'd taken off his clothes for her—but that time she'd run from him and kept on running.

Fool, she berated herself, regretting the days and nights she'd wasted in trying to avoid the inevitable.

This time she didn't run. Not even when he stepped out of his trousers and peeled away his underwear, and revealed the sculpted perfection of his body. Every last glorious inch of him.

This time she wasn't running anywhere. Already her body was preparing for their next encounter. She slipped off her shoes and, kneeling on the bed, slid down the zip on her dress. She let the straps fall from her shoulders, the weight of the skirt pulling it past her waist and down to pool around her knees, leaving her naked before him apart from her stockings.

His choked gasp of appreciation fed into her psyche, further fuelling her unaccustomed shamelessness. She leant down, and touched a hand to the lace top of one stocking.

'Leave them,' he insisted, joining her on the bed and untangling her from the circle of her dress as he ran his hands up the shimmering length of her legs. 'I've been dreaming about these all week.'

More words she didn't need to hear. Not when after tonight she'd be walking away. But she tossed the misgiving away, refusing to let it spoil the magic of this night, the magic of what he was doing to her nipples with his mouth and hands right now, and the magic feel of him pressing between her thighs once again.

After tonight there could be no more dreaming. But at least she had tonight. At least she would have memories.

'Stay with me for the weekend.'

She rolled her head away. 'I can't. I have plans.'

'Cancel them,' he said gruffly. He'd never known a night like it. They'd made love and then shared a spa; he'd pleasured her with his mouth, and then she'd more than returned the favour, and still they'd fallen into each other's arms when they'd returned to bed. Now they'd just woken up to great sex. Why should it end now? The weekend was just a pup.

'I can't.'

'I'm sure you'll find a way,' he said, biting back on a much earthier retort. 'I have much better plans in mind for the weekend.'

She just shook her head. 'I'm sorry.'

He latched his mouth onto the nearest nipple and drew it in deep, taking a different form of attack. She'd proven how responsive she was to his touch last night. She trembled in response, but still managed to shrug him away. 'Please don't do that. I really have to go.'

'Why?'

'I told you,' she said, gathering a sheet around her as she left the bed. 'I have plans.'

'Which don't include me.' It wasn't a question.

'That's about the size of it, yes.'

He sat up, the good feeling he'd had all night sluicing away into a bowl of disgruntlement. 'So what's so damn important you can't cancel it?'

She looked around for her underwear, then gave up and simply shrugged her dress over her head, dropping the sheet on the floor as she wriggled into the dress and zipped it up.

'My sister's coming home from holidays. I have to pick her up from the airport.'

'I'll take you,' he decided. 'I'd like to meet her.'

'*No!*'

Her reply was so vehement that it stopped him in his tracks. 'You don't want me to meet your sister?'

'There's no need, that's all.'

'Then maybe we can hook up later.'

'No.'

'Tomorrow?'

'I don't think so.' She pulled on her shoes, stuffing her stockings into her bag. The fact she couldn't be bothered to put them on when he was watching—pull that long length of glistening nylon up those legs after he'd had the pleasure of pulling them down—was the *last* straw.

He rounded the bed. 'What's going on here?'

'Nothing's going on. Why should it be?'

'Then what's wrong?'

'Look. I just can't stay with you, okay? And I can't see you again.'

'But what about last night?'

'What about last night? I had too much to drink. You scratched an itch. Consenting adults and all that. It didn't mean anything. Okay?'

His hackles were way up. 'You didn't have too much to drink. You were the one who asked me to make love—remember?'

She stood rigid, the green flecks in her hazel eyes sharp like daggers. 'Does that sound like something the Morgan who's worked with you for the last eighteen months would do?'

'No… But—'

'You see? I'd had too much to drink. Too much to celebrate. I'm sorry, Maverick, I'll call a taxi and wait outside.

'I'll take you ho—'

'Please,' she said, holding up one hand. 'We have to

work together. I think it's better for both of us if I just get a taxi and we don't prolong this, don't you?'

A muscle in his cheek twitched, the skin of his face suddenly looking too tight, too severely stretched over the planes and angles of his face. 'Yes.' He nodded. 'I think you're absolutely right.'

She wasn't going to cry. She sat sullenly in the cab all the way home, determined not to give in to tears while the cab driver ignored her need for silence and insisted on delivering a non-stop monologue about the lack of rain, the price of fuel and how to solve the Middle East crisis.

Thankfully he seemed to be happy with her grunt of assent every now and then, because she didn't want to think about the weather, the drought or the crisis in the Middle East. Right now she had her own crisis to take care of, given the look of dark thunder Maverick had thrown at her as she'd walked out the door.

He was angry with her, furious at her for turning him down, for spending a night of pleasure with him and then leaving him cold. But what choice did she have?

It was better this way, better that he hated her and thought her flaky. He'd leave her alone now after what she'd done—leave *Morgan* alone come Monday morning! And that was what was important.

She let herself into her flat, wanting nothing more than a long, hot bath until she had to head to the airport to pick up her sister, when she noticed the flashing light on her answering machine.

Warily she approached it. Maverick, she guessed, Maverick unable as ever to take no for an answer.

But still she felt compelled to press the play button.

There were two messages, it told her. *Message one…* She steeled herself for Maverick's strident tones, had almost allowed herself to relax, when she recognised her sister's usual greeting—until the next part of her message worked its way into Tegan's sleep-deprived psyche…

'I hope you're getting on better with Maverick now because I'm afraid I might be over here a bit longer than anticipated…'

CHAPTER EIGHT

TEGAN reeled as her sister's words sunk in—*a tourist-bus crash...nobody seriously hurt...slight matter of a broken leg...about to be wheeled into surgery...*

Surgery? That no doubt accounted for the brittle quality to her sister's voice. Morgan sounded like she was still in shock or high on medication or both.

The second message began. It was from Jake, one of the party she was travelling with. Morgan was out of surgery, he said, and wanted her to know she'd come through with flying colours. But she'd had multiple fractures which had required pinning, and she wouldn't be travelling for several weeks at least. And Morgan had especially wanted her to know that she was really sorry.

Tegan collapsed into a chair. Her sister was okay, thank God, but she so wished she'd been home to take the call and talk to Morgan herself before she'd had to go under the anaesthetic. But she hadn't been home. Instead of being here to take her twin's call, she'd been out making love all night with her twin's boss.

Tegan dropped her head into her hands. Oh hell, what a mess! Morgan wasn't travelling anywhere for weeks. Which meant Morgan wouldn't magically be re-appearing to take over her job come Monday. What the hell was Tegan supposed to do now—pretend to be Morgan and try to work with Maverick for another how ever many weeks?

Oh, dear God, no!

Oh, sure, she'd managed to convince him she was Morgan so far, but she could hardly consider her efforts a victory, more like survival. And so far, apart from a night of memories that would stay with her for ever, she'd escaped from it all with nothing.

Least of all her self-respect.

She couldn't continue with the farce. Her deal with Morgan had been for one week only, and that had been with Maverick half a world away. Already she'd gone above and beyond the call of duty.

Already the lie was too big, too damaging, the repercussions and consequences growing nastier by the day.

She had no choice but to come clean. Morgan would probably lose her job because if it, but Maverick was bound to find out the truth sooner or later. Better it came from Tegan now.

All she had to do was work out a way to tell him.

He'd spent all weekend stewing. He wasn't going to call her. There was no point. If she could walk out on him after a night like they'd shared together, then she wasn't worth the effort. He was over it.

He looked at his watch and growled. So where was she?

Then he heard the lift doors ping, and his gut pulled tighter than a drum.

One infinitely long minute later and she was there, knocking lightly at the open door.

He barely flicked his eyes in her direction. 'You're late.' She took a step in, and out of the corner of his eye he detected her heels waver shakily on the carpet.

'Maverick, I need to talk to you.' It gave him a fair chunk of satisfaction that her grip on the earth wasn't the only thing that was wobbly. He leant back in his chair and put his hands behind his neck. This was going to be good.

'Have a nice weekend with your sister?'

Her lips compressed into a tight line as she crossed her arms low over her chest. Her whole face seemed pinched, and even her hazel eyes looked clouded. Yet still he couldn't chase away the vision of her, warm and receptive, and clad in nothing more than a pair of sheer silken stockings to guide him home.

'She didn't make it. She got held up.'

He grunted. That was no surprise. It had just been an excuse to get away from him.

She took another shaky step into his office, winding a loose tendril of hair back around her ear, and contemplating the floor as though any moment she wanted it to swallow her up. He couldn't help but bristle. Was she really so cut up because she'd spent a night in the boss's bed? From what he remembered, it sure hadn't seemed that it'd been an episode in endurance for her. Surely there were worse things in the world?

'I almost didn't come in at all today,' she started. 'I was going to call, but I figured you deserved to hear what I have to say face to face.'

'You don't have an option about whether or not you come in. You have a contract to work here, remember?'

But she just smiled strangely and shook her head. 'No. I'm sorry to let you down—to let everyone down. But I just can't do this any more.'

He launched himself out of his chair and rounded the desk towards her. 'What do you mean, "can't do this any more"? Just because of what happened Friday night? Don't you think you're overreacting? "Consenting adults" and all that.' He spat her own words back at her—words that had been eating into his gut all weekend like an acid burn. She had consented—that was the point—so why had she cut and run?

She flinched at his words and his tone, jerking her chin up as she swallowed, and her eyes sparked icicles as for once they sought him out as he circled her like a shark.

'It's not just about what happened Friday.'

'Then what are you afraid of?' he asked as he rounded her back.

Her head swivelled around to meet his once more. 'I'm not afraid!'

'Then why are you running away?'

'You don't understand—'

'You didn't enjoy spending the night with me?'

'That's not the point.'

'So you did enjoy it.'

'What is this? Did I bruise your ego when I didn't beg for a repeat performance?'

His dark eyes turned from rich chocolate to boiling mud pools in a second, and she kicked herself for letting herself be distracted from her task.

'Maverick...' she pleaded.

A phone interrupted them, sharp and insistent. 'That'll be Rogerson,' he said, sweeping up his mobile phone from his desk. 'I'm expecting this call. We'll continue this discussion later.'

'There's nothing to discuss.'

'Later!'

He turned his back to her, and still she remained where she was, until it was clear that he expected her to fade into the woodwork and take her issues with her. Finally she wheeled around and fumed back to her desk.

Damn the man! She should have phoned after all. It would have been easier. At least then she wouldn't have been subjected to that lazy gaze that looked like dark chocolate and felt rapier sharp. And she wouldn't have been distracted by his threatening proximity.

Why was she arguing with him about whether or not she'd enjoyed their love making, for heaven's sake? She was supposed to have been admitting that for the last week she'd been doing this job under false pretences, not goading him with challenges to his virility.

As soon as he came out she would put him straight. No more distractions. No more beating around the bush. Just the facts.

She bet her wanting to leave wouldn't be an issue after that. He'd probably throw her out himself.

'Grab your things,' Maverick snapped out, taking her by surprise as he suddenly emerged from his office. 'We've got a meeting at Rogerson's in fifteen minutes.'

'Maverick, we haven't finished—'

'We have now. He's waiting for us. He's put his project team together and wants us all to get together.'

'No. Hang on and listen. This is important. Because I'm not—'

'On the team?' He cut her off. 'You are now.

Rogerson's insisting he wants you on it, especially after that job you did with the project-development chart. And, given I'll probably be unavailable on some days, it makes sense you be there. So I've agreed.'

She clawed her hands in frustration. 'But I haven't agreed! You haven't listened to one thing I've said today.'

'You're upset,' he said. 'You'll get over it. Come on.'

'Don't you dare patronise me.'

He stopped then and wheeled around in a semi-circle. 'Rogerson's asked for you to be on the team. You *personally*. Now if you've got a problem with that, if you want to let this project down, maybe you should discuss it with him.'

'My problem isn't with Phil Rogerson,' she hissed.

'Fine,' he said. 'We can discuss any little problems we have later. But, for right now, let's go.'

She was trapped. Her head pounding, her heart thumping, she let herself be shepherded back into Maverick's car, clicking herself into the seat belt on autopilot, while all the time chewing on her bottom lip. The meeting had been a blur. Apart from when Phil Rogerson had insisted she be part of the Royalty Cove team. That part of the meeting had been vividly playing over and over again in her mind's eye with crystal-clear clarity.

"I want you on board for the entire project," he'd told her, his creased face smiling into hers, his work-callused hands surrounding hers. "You're someone I feel I can trust, and I know you're going to be a valuable member of the team. I know you won't let us down."

And she'd nodded dumbly, and all the while had felt

sick to the stomach, because she wasn't deserving of anyone's trust, least of all Phil Rogerson's. She was a liar, caught in the web of her own deceit, a web that was spreading, wider and stickier by the minute. She was a spider, no more than a dumb spider stuck in its own trap.

How could she possibly make things better with a simple confession now? She couldn't. Not without making things a whole lot worse—for everyone.

What the hell was she going to do?

'You're very quiet.'

She blinked and looked around as Maverick's words floated down through the leaden weight of her thoughts, surprised to find they'd come to a halt in a parking bay fringed with Norfolk Island pines adjacent to the beach. She hadn't even registered that he'd left the highway, let alone parked the car.

'Why are we here?'

He wasn't really sure. Except it had something to do with not wanting to return to the battle ground of the office just yet. He was in no hurry to resume where they'd left off this morning.

And, damn it, being with her again just one short morning had been enough to tell him he wasn't finished with her yet. There was no way he wanted to do battle with her, unless it involved tearing off her clothes and getting horizontal.

Which, come to think of it, was one of the best ideas he'd had all morning...

'I thought we could do with some fresh air,' he told her. 'Care for a walk along the beach?'

She looked at him like he was mad. 'What's going on?'

'Come on,' he urged, slinging his jacket in the back seat and rolling up his sleeves. 'It will do us both good.'

Ten minutes later she had sand between her stockinged toes and salt spray in her hair. It was utter madness, strolling along the beach dressed for the office, but today she didn't care. The sun was shining; the breeze carried with it the clean, fresh tang of the ocean and the rhythm of the waves swooshing up the beach was like a balm to her soul.

She stole a glance at the man walking alongside her. Like her, he held his shoes in one hand, the legs of his trousers rolled up and his naked feet leaving impressions on the sand. My God, she thought, even his feet were sexy.

But then it wasn't anything that she hadn't learned on Friday night, just one of a whole host of discoveries she'd made that evening: what his skin felt like and where, the difference between rough and smooth, of satiny skin dusted with springy hair, of what he liked her to do to him and what he was so good and so generous at giving.

Heat welled up inside her at the memories, deliciously different from the sun's warming rays from the outside; this was a compelling heat that set her flesh alive with the echoes of how he'd made her feel that night.

He looked across at her, and their eyes snagged and locked, his meeting her turmoil-filled gaze with a deeply contemplative one, before she stopped and broke contact, afraid of revealing too much. She turned her eyes out to sea, gulping in air like someone who'd been under one too many times.

Which is exactly how she felt. She was drowning in the complexities of a lie she could see no way out of.

And meanwhile she was drowning in physical sensations she had no right to experience.

Life couldn't get any crazier.

He came to a halt alongside her as she watched the waves come in. She was fascinated by the smooth slide of water over sand, wishing her own life could move so seemingly effortlessly.

'You agreed to join Rogerson's dream team today.'

At last, she thought, at last we get to the point of this expedition.

'So it seems.'

'In which case you've obviously abandoned the idea of leaving.'

Her shoes jostled nervously together against her hip. It was nothing she didn't know already, but hearing him say the words made it infinitely more real. How could she leave now? It was no longer just her sister who had expectations of her. It wasn't only Maverick. The net was now cast wider. Phil Rogerson had tied her to the project for the duration.

She gritted her teeth together as seagulls circled and cawed overhead, and the endless waves rolled in and slipped back out. This was no longer just a case of coming clean and cutting her losses and worrying about whether Morgan had a job to come back to. There would be serious fallout now. There would be consequences.

And maybe all she could do was try to minimise them. Which meant she had to keep up the pretence, to hold on to this job until Morgan returned. And to try to hold on to her sanity in the process.

She sighed. 'It looks like it.'

He said nothing for a while, and she thought she'd

made a mistake, that there had never been a point to his questions and that he'd just been making conversation to cover the yawning vacuum between them.

Until he stepped between her, and the view and her vision was filled by a man whose dark looks were so heavy with savage intent that one look put her brain on high alert and left her senses smouldering. 'In that case,' he said, 'I have a proposition for you.'

She looked up at him, already drowning in his eyes, already feeling the pull of his body on hers, already anticipating the slide of skin against skin—while her brain screamed warnings, warnings that made a whole lot of sense right now.

She shook her head, and made a move to step out of range of his intense eyes and back along the beach. 'Oh, no, I don't think so.'

He grabbed her wrist, and she jerked with the shock, spilling her shoes to the sand.

'You haven't even heard what it is yet.'

She looked up at him, and at all that his tortured features proclaimed. She didn't need to hear it. She could read it in his anguished expression. 'I won't sleep with you.'

He drew himself up, his eyes narrowing, and she knew she'd guessed right. But still he didn't let go of her wrist. Instead he tugged her ever so gently towards him. 'But you already have.'

'It was a mistake. It should never have happened.'

'I wish all my mistakes were so satisfying. And you were satisfying—in *every* way.'

She wrenched her eyes away, turning them up to the sky, a silent entreaty. *Oh God, no, don't tell me that.* 'Look, Maverick, I just think we should forget about it.'

'That's my problem,' he argued, letting his shoes drop to the sand and sliding his hand down her elbow to capture her free hand in his. 'I can't forget about it. I can't forget how you felt next to me, how good you tasted in my mouth and how good it felt to bury myself deep inside you.'

His words, erotically charged, shockingly intimate, brought the memories of that night bubbling up in both her mind and her body in a heated rush, rendering her speechless as muscle after hidden muscle relived the feel of accepting him.

'And the way I can feel your pulse racing right now,' he continued, 'I don't think you can forget it either.'

'I'm being harassed on a public beach,' she protested in barely a breathless whisper that she knew sounded like no protest at all. 'Of course my pulse is racing!'

'And I suppose your nipples always peak like that too, when you're being harassed?'

Only when I'm being harassed by you.

She swallowed back the retort that would have told him far too much. Shame at her body's unavoidable reaction to him burned her cheeks. There was no point denying the truth.

'You want me,' he continued, leisurely running his hands up her arms in a heated caress. 'And, God knows, I want you. Why should we deny ourselves what we know we both want?'

'Because it's not that simple.'

'Why isn't it that simple? You as good as said there was nobody else.'

'It's not that,' she said truthfully, because she knew it was infinitely worse than that—she simply *was* someone else. But what reason might Maverick understand?

'I work for you,' she argued. 'And I don't think that bonking the boss is necessarily a wise career strategy.'

He put a finger under her chin and tilted her face up towards his. 'Is that what you're worried about—that you might lose your job when it's over?'

'When what's over? Nothing's even begun!'

'Oh, yes,' he said. 'It's begun. And it's not going to go away all by itself. Why are you making this so difficult?'

'I'm trying to be sensible.'

'No, you're just being provocative. The more you run, the more I have to chase.'

'So, how do I get you to stop chasing?'

'Simple. By letting this thing between us run its course.'

'Oh, right. I become your mistress for however long, and then what happens? I somehow go back to being PA pure and simple, and you go back to being the boss from hell, and we both pretend it never happened?'

'Just like it never happened,' he repeated, ignoring her jibe. 'But if I don't get you out of my system I swear I'm going to go mad, and it's going to be hell trying to work together.'

She believed it. It had been bad enough for a week before they'd made love. Now, knowing what they'd experienced together, and exactly what they'd be missing out on, it would be intolerable. Which was exactly the reason she'd decided to come clean this morning and put an end to the torture.

But leaving wasn't an option any more.

Did he really believe things could go back to anywhere near normal after having an affair together, after sharing more of the kind of intimacies they'd already enjoyed?

But if he did…

If it were possible…

Maybe there was a chance.

She breathed in, and the smell of beach and sand and sea, and the unmistakable tang of desire, filled her lungs while sultry thoughts invaded her mind.

'So how long…?' she started nervously. 'How long do you think it might take to *get me out of your system*?'

He gave a careless shrug that belied the glimmer of imminent victory she saw flare to life in his eyes. 'Two weeks, maybe three.'

'Wow,' she said, trying to be light, but knowing it was going to take one heck of a lot longer for her to forget him in a hurry. 'That long.'

'Hey,' he growled, putting his hands on her shoulders. 'You asked. And I'm trying to be honest up front. I don't do long term.'

'So you're saying the sooner we get started, the sooner we get each other out of our systems, the sooner we can get back to how things used to be?'

'That's about the size of it.'

The waves rolled in. Joggers splashed through the shallows and moved on. The sun continued to shine down. Everything was the same and yet everything was different, and her crazy day had just defied all odds and got even crazier.

Nothing could dissuade her from the thought that the idea had some merit. Morgan was gone for maybe six weeks. And until she came back Tegan could undertake the duties on Phil Rogerson's team as she'd agreed. She could continue to perform her sister's role as Maverick's PA by day and occupy his sheets by night. And, by the time Morgan came back, this brief affair would have burned out and the fires long grown cold.

She could be the good sister, the good employee, and she could safely satisfy his needs and her own desires at the same time.

It was the answer to everything.

It was perfect.

'In that case,' she said, turning her face up towards him, the unmitigated thrill of anticipation setting her flesh to tingling, 'maybe the sooner we get started, the better.'

Had he been a lion, he would have roared his victory from on high for all the world to hear. As it was, the blood rushing in his ears served the same purpose—a crashing roar that heralded a victory, a triumphant roar of possession.

She came into his arms more than willingly, and as his mouth descended upon hers he knew she was his for as long as he wanted her. It was everything that he wanted.

It was everything he had craved.

And Morgan was no conniving bitch. He knew she was no more like Tina than summer was like snow. This time it would be different. This time he was making no mistakes.

He drank her in, right there on the beach, inhaling her perfume, supping on her essence. She'd run from him before, but she was no longer running. She was his for the taking. And he intended to take all he could while he could.

He broke the kiss, his chest heaving, his breathing out of control, knowing only too well that a public beach was no forum for the type of culmination to this activity that he had in mind.

He looked down into her flushed face, her glazed eyes and kiss-plumped lips. 'What's in the diary for the rest of the day?'

Warm hazel eyes shone back up at him, their intention clear. 'Nothing I can't reschedule.'

It was the right answer. He smiled his approval and gathered her in the crook of his arm before heading back along the beach towards the car. Business could wait. Today he had much higher priorities.

CHAPTER NINE

IT WAS a world she'd never dreamed existed, like living in a fantasy. Days and nights blurred into one long, sensual experience, with meals becoming orgies of the senses, with work becoming a journey of discovery into new and interesting ways to use office furniture.

Tegan loved the way he made her feel, loved the way he could so easily arouse her, loved nothing more than when he drove himself home inside her and brought her to completion.

And then at night he'd insist she dress up in clothes he'd had delivered especially from the best boutiques, and he'd wine and dine her in the best restaurants on the strip, then afterwards he'd take her to his island house with the glass walls and he'd make love to her all over again.

Never had the idea of going to the office been more appealing. And never had dressing for the office been more fun. Because now she wasn't interested in repelling him, so she'd abandoned Morgan's severe suits and pencil skirts. Now she dressed in soft fabrics that showed off her figure and teased Maverick to distraction. Now she dressed for easy access. And easy removal.

It was two o'clock in the afternoon, and Tegan leant back amongst the bubbles of the deep spa-bath and closed her eyes, letting the jets work their magic on muscles and flesh wearied by another matinee love-making session while she waited for Maverick to join her.

He was such a wonderful lover, she could almost forgive him his relentless pursuit of success. Almost. It was a shame they were such different people, because one day she'd love nothing more than to find a good man who could make her feel this wonderful perma-nently, not just for the length of a fling.

'You look good enough to eat.'

She opened her eyes to see him standing there watching her, his eyes at her breasts, where they bobbed through the water's surface, their pink tips fringed with foam. Her nipples peaked as he watched her, his body similarly stirring into action.

So he was a heartless businessman, she thought; a girl could do a lot worse than having a fling with a man called Maverick. She smiled up at him and held out one hand. 'So eat me,' she said.

It was a day or two later that he gave her the first gift. A blue box appeared on her pillow. 'What's this?' she asked.

'Just a little trinket,' he answered.

'You don't have to buy me things.'

'I know. Open it.'

'No,' she said, holding it out to him. 'I mean it. You've already showered me with clothes. I don't want you buying me more. There's no point to it.'

'You don't like jewellery?'

'I don't need it. And it just seems such a waste,

when there are people in the world who can't afford to eat and you just splash money around as if it doesn't matter.'

'It doesn't matter. Not to me.'

'But there are people who have absolutely nothing but a few cooking pots and the hope that one day they'll have something to put in them. Couldn't you do something more constructive with your money than buy worthless presents for me?'

'When did you suddenly develop a social conscience?' he argued impatiently, ripping open the box and pulling out the contents, a gold Tiffany necklace that took her breath away. 'I bought you this because I wanted to. Indulge me.'

'But, Maverick—' she said, still protesting even as he did up the clasp behind her neck.

'*And* because I want you to wear it when we make love…' He pushed her back into the pillows, insinuating himself between her thighs and positioning the pendant with his fingers to exactly the right place between her breasts. 'So that every time you wear it you think of me, doing this…'

She gasped as he entered her, filling her completely as his dark eyes held hers captive, withdrawing only to slam into her again, building the momentum, driving into her relentlessly, never letting her eyes escape until he'd blown her into starburst.

Two weeks he'd said it would last. Maybe three. But already it had been all of that and his passion showed no sign of abating. They worked together during the day. They slept together at night. But they only achieved either one of them when they weren't making love.

And her greatest fear had taken on a new and frightening dimension. Now it wasn't a question of how soon this thing between them would burn out, but whether it would burn out in time.

Tegan lay propped up on her elbows on Maverick's big bed, watching the steady rise and fall of the chest of the man lying beside her. Morning light filtered through the curtains, turning his bare skin into a study of light and shadow and sheer masculine beauty. She studied his face—the shadowed jaw, the generous mouth, the dark tangle of lashes and brows—and a sizzle of realisation moved through her like a lightning bolt that sucked the air from her chest along with it.

No, whether this thing burned out before Morgan's return wasn't her greatest problem at all.

Her problem was far more complicated than that.

Her problem now was that she didn't want it to end.

God, she was a fool! She'd known she'd be playing with fire when she'd agreed to this deal. She might have tried to convince herself that she was doing Morgan some kind of favour by becoming her boss's mistress, but Tegan's motives had been purely selfish. She simply hadn't been able to resist.

With a sigh she let her head drop back down into the crook of his arm, drinking in the musky scent of male he wore so well while she still could.

Later today he was leaving with Phil Rogerson for Milan to tie up the contract with Zeppabanca once and for all, and even the thought of being parted from him for just a few days was hard enough to bear. How much worse would the sick feeling in her stomach be when he left her for good?

And leave her he would, regardless of what she

wanted. He'd as much as promised it. Already she was on borrowed time, and Maverick would drop her cold when it suited him. She was just going to have to deal with the fallout when it happened.

The man beside her stirred. An arm snaked over her and hauled her against his chest with a growl, as warm lips nuzzled against her forehead and a warmer palm found her breast.

'Maybe you should come to Milan with me after all.' His fingers teased her sensitive nipple into hardness, while the other hand cupped one cheek of her behind, dragging her closer to his growing hardness.

She laughed thinly, half wishing it could be so, knowing full well it couldn't be, and only thankful he hadn't insisted on her accompanying him from the start. 'You don't need me to sign a few documents. I'll be here when you get back.'

'Then make sure you are.' He pressed his mouth to hers, and for a few seconds she was half convinced she could travel on her own passport in her sister's name, make it work and to hell with the consequences.

'What time's my flight again?'

'Eleven-fifteen.'

'Then we have time,' he said, before rolling her beneath him once again.

Tegan had just returned to the office from her lunch break when the call came.

'I'm sorry to call you at the office, Tiggy. Is it okay to talk? I left messages at home for you and I was starting to get worried.'

'I'm sorry,' Tegan said, shoving her lunchtime acqui-sition away in her bag with a sickening stab of panic, not to mention guilt. She'd spent most of her nights lately at Maverick's house with not a thought to how her sister was getting on, and if she'd been trying to contact her. 'I've been…kind of busy. But it's okay to talk now. How's the leg?'

'You won't believe it! The doctors are hoping they'll be able to send me home by Christmas. I can't wait to get out of here, and so soon, I can tell you.'

Christmas. Three weeks away. She'd always known that this affair wouldn't last, and indeed couldn't last beyond Morgan's return, but having an end date made it so much more real. One way or another the affair would have to end by then. 'Wow, that is soon.'

'Yeah, I knew you'd be relieved. You must be so sick of Maverick by now.'

'It's not that bad. He's in Italy at the moment. Gone to seal that deal at last.'

'That must be a relief. You won't have to put up with him for too much longer, then.'

Did her sister have to remind her?

'And Maverick still has no idea you're not me?'

'I think I've managed to take his mind off any subtle differences between us—yeah.'

She could almost hear her sister's smile of appreciation down the phone line.

'Thanks so much, Tiggy. You're a fantastic sister for doing what you're doing. You're a star.'

Tegan wanted to argue about the 'fantastic sister' angle. She was sure Morgan wouldn't be saying it if she knew how well she was getting on with the boss. But instead she merely gave a noncommittal answer as guilt wrapped around her anew.

Morgan didn't deserve to come home to a mess like this—a mess that Tegan prayed wasn't about to get any more complicated. But she was probably worrying unnecessarily. She was only two days late after all, and her periods had been all over the place since that virus had hit her. Besides, they'd always used protection. The chances were next to nil. She wasn't going to panic about it yet, and she most certainly wasn't going to worry Morgan into the deal.

Because as much as she longed to be able to share what she was going through, her doubts and her fears, it would hardly be fair. Morgan was so far away, and still recovering from a road accident.

So she turned the conversation to hospitals and Hawaii and anything else that might steer the conversation away from Maverick, and the methods her twin sister was really employing to distract him.

The Zeppabanca deal was done, the papers signed, and the first-class service on the flight back was as usual unobtrusively impeccable. Maverick pressed back in the wide seat and stretched out his legs. All was right with the world.

And in a few short hours he'd be home and things were going to get even better. Five days away had honed his need to razor sharp.

Alongside him Phil Rogerson sighed as he folded his newspaper and dropped it onto his table beside his Scotch and water. 'It's been a good trip, but I'm looking forward to getting home.'

Maverick nodded. *Oh, yes!* He had a pair of hazel eyes to meet him at the airport, not to mention a pair of sensationally long legs he was eager to feel wrapping around him not long after. Legs hopefully wearing those lace-topped stockings.

Rogerson took a slug of his Scotch. 'Only the jetlag to deal with now, of course.'

The other man grunted. He was planning on burying his jetlag while he was busy burying himself in Morgan. When he collapsed into sleep tonight, it wouldn't be because he'd changed time zones, that was a certainty.

'Oh, I meant to say,' Phil continued. 'I've got a car picking me up at the airport, so if you need a lift…'

'Thanks,' he acknowledged. 'But I've made arrangements.'

'Morgan picking you up?'

Maverick regarded him levelly. 'As it happens, yes.'

Rogerson nodded. 'I have a lot of respect for that young woman. And admiration. You're a lucky man.'

Wanting to set Rogerson to rights battled with an insane stab of jealousy. 'She's my PA,' he said flatly. 'That's all.'

The other man contemplated Maverick, one bushy eyebrow arched up high. 'Ah, I obviously had the wrong end of the stick.'

'Employees and long-term relationships are not a good-news story as far as I'm concerned.'

'Really? It's never been something that bothered me. Mind you, maybe that's because I married the office junior myself. And, even though I was the boss, it still took me a good six months to work up the courage to ask her out. We'll be married forty-five years next February.' The older man sighed. 'Doris turned out to be the best thing that ever happened to me.'

Maverick shook his head. 'Too risky for me.'

'You know, I think that's one of the first things that

convinced me that Morgan is special. She doesn't hang back, she doesn't advocate being safe. When I was prevaricating over whether or not to go ahead with the deal, it was her words that convinced me. She told me that there are times when it's worth going out on a limb, it's worth taking a risk. She was right in my case too.' He handed his glass to a passing flight attendant as the 'fasten seat belt' sign came on in preparation for landing. 'My word, she's a gutsy girl all right.'

Maverick wasn't sure he disagreed. What baffled him was why it had taken him so long to notice.

Tegan stood in the crowded arrivals lounge, her nerves stretched tighter than fencing wire, her stomach home to a swarm of dragon flies—drunken dragonflies, that crashed into the walls of her gut and slid down only to relaunch themselves into intoxicated flight once more, the odd one catching her squarely in the lungs.

When she'd received Maverick's email to pick him up from the airport her heart had skipped a beat. The fact that he wanted to see her as soon as he returned had to mean that he wasn't finished with her yet. And in spite of everything the notion warmed her more than it should, spreading through her bones like a drug.

Because she wanted to see him too. She didn't want him to come back and decide that he was over her. She wanted the opportunity of making love to him once more, just one last time, before she broke her news.

Just one last time; that wasn't too much to ask, surely? And then the cards could lie where they fell. And all of them—Morgan, Tegan and Maverick— would just have to live with the consequences.

The arrivals doors slid open and her tall, dark corporate cowboy strode through, his briefcase in one hand, luggage suspended in the other.

Her heart gave a little leap as their eyes connected, and it felt for a moment like every part of her smiled, though she didn't make a move towards him. She was content for now just to drink him in.

Maverick.

Her Maverick. So it wouldn't be for ever. So it would soon be over. But he'd been hers for a while. A thrill of secret pleasure zipped up her spine.

Because, whatever happened, *now she had something of him to keep for ever*.

Something that would make her lonely days apart from him worthwhile. Something that would ease the pain of losing the man she loved.

Not even the scary prospect of being a partnerless single mother, unemployed and without her own home, could snuff out the sheer spark of delight she felt because she was carrying Maverick's child. Always she would have part of him to hold dear. And she would cope. She had the money saved up from her work overseas, plus her share of her father's modest estate when it settled. She could do it.

He came closer, the father of her child, bearing the unmistakeable imprint of long-haul air travel, and yet unlike on most people it only served to make him look even sexier. The shadow at his jaw was evidence of hours away from a razor; his wavy hair looked more rumpled. But still his eyes looked down at her, darkly dangerous, his mouth turned up in a lazy smile, and every cell in her body became an exercise in anticipation as expectation sizzled into life inside her.

Then he turned and spoke and the moment splintered, and she was left confused and floundering as the noise of meet and greets and the jostle of movement and colour returned—and for the first time she noticed the man who'd stepped through the doors alongside him.

'Hello, Morgan,' Phil said, his creased face tired and somehow sympathetic. 'My car's waiting outside. I guess I'll see you both some time soon.'

Then he was gone and it was Maverick looking into her face, his brow slightly furrowed, his eyes perplexed.

He smiled, and the warmth from his eyes flowed right down to her toes. 'Take me home,' he said.

'Do you want to drive?' she asked when they got to Morgan's neat Honda coupé and opened the boot for his luggage.

He just turfed the luggage in and shook his head. Then he gave that look in her direction again that set her alight, and the soles of her shoes all but melted. 'Today I want the full five-star treatment.'

She swallowed; sure as hell he wasn't referring to her driving, and her plans were rapidly going south. Tonight was ultimately supposed to be get-serious time. She had news to share, and then a confession that must be made. There was no choice now, regardless of the fallout, regardless of what might happen to Morgan's job or her own reputation, or anything—the stakes were suddenly too high, too damning.

But if he kept on looking at her that way, like she actually meant something more to him than a convenient mistress, then there was no way she wanted to spoil that feeling. Not just yet.

And she knew that was wrong.

It was a heady journey, Maverick filling her passenger seat angled towards her, too big, too warm and all too male, his fingers lazily toying with the ends of her hair as she tried to concentrate on driving and not how he was making her feel.

His fingers dipped to her neck, tracing the sweep of skin across her collarbone to her singlet straps, caressing her shoulder, following it with a press of his lips. She inhaled his scent, familiar and welcome once more. 'I missed you,' he said. 'I missed the feel of your skin against mine.'

She shivered into his caress, looking forward to what would happen when they got to his house, clamping down on unwelcome fears about what the aftermath would bring.

'I missed these…'

His hand lightly cupped one breast, teasing her breast into delicious fullness, teasing an already sensitive nipple into exquisite tightness before dropping to her knee, sliding under her skirt and up her leg.

She gasped, thankful for light traffic and automatic gears, and never more thankful that they were not far from their destination.

'And I really missed…' his fingertips rounded her thigh, brushing the moist place between '…*this*.'

It was shockingly intimate. Devastatingly effective.

It was out and out crazy.

'Maverick!' she pleaded, never for a moment thinking he'd go so far. 'You can't do that! I'm trying to drive here.'

She tried to push his arm away, but the attempt was half-hearted at best—she liked how he was making her feel, she liked being the epicentre of his world—so she gave it up as a bad joke. Besides, she was better off right now keeping both hands on the wheel.

But it was madness. Already she could feel ripples of pleasure starting to build inside as her flesh reacted, only too keen to make up for their forced abstinence.

'Can't you drive any faster?' he asked as his fingers teased her mercilessly, his lips and tongue busy at her shoulder.

'I'm already doing the speed limit,' she said, her words little more than a breathy whisper as he continued to pleasure her. Waves and waves of pleasure. Maybe she should pull over and let him finish this thing, but in a highly erotic way this was better. This was forbidden and dangerous and impossible, in fact all those things Maverick had always been.

She braked gently and he looked up. 'What now?'

'Red light,' she explained, and he growled his satisfaction.

'Perfect.'

She'd barely brought the car to a halt, still with enough sense to jerk on the handbrake, when his fingers slid underneath her panties to circle that tight, aching bud until she was ready to explode. He dragged her face around and pulled her into a kiss that threatened to devour her with his hunger and need. And he slipped his fingers lower and pressed two fingers into her slickness, his thumb not neglecting that sweet, tight spot, and she did explode, right there in the driver's seat of the car.

It was crazy. It was insane. So maybe it wasn't rush hour and there wasn't a lot of traffic—but it was still broad daylight on a sunny Sunday on the main thoroughfare through the Gold Coast, and he'd made her come while they'd waited for the traffic lights to change.

'You missed me,' he said as he straightened her skirt, and she could hear the satisfaction in his voice.

She took a couple of deep breaths while her breathing steadied. 'How could you tell?'

He chuckled as the light turned green. She pressed her languid muscles into work and stepped on the accelerator.

Later it was like that first time all over again. Once on the island they didn't make it to the front door before he was driving into her, blowing her senses and raising her hopes.

Maybe it won't be so bad, she thought as he powered into her like a machine, a marvelous machine of muscled perfection that had been crafted just to pleasure her. Maybe he wouldn't react badly to her news. Maybe he might forgive her for deceiving him all this time.

Maybe...

Then he took her high again, to that place where rhyme and reason no longer existed, and she abandoned all concerns about the future as she went with him, spinning into a world of sensation where there existed nothing but the two of them and a blanket of a million stars to wrap around them.

'Here we go.' Maverick placed glasses and an ice bucket down on a side table. Inside the ice bucket the neck of a bottle of Dom Perignon leaned jauntily to one side. Outside the light was fading, and night would soon close around them.

Tegan lay on her stomach and watched him dispense with the foil and wire and release the cork, a feeling of sadness swamping the joy she'd felt in the hours since they'd come back from the airport. She'd known ever since she'd picked him up that she could no longer put off the truth, but here he was presenting her with the perfect opportunity to admit her pregnancy.

He handed her a flute filled with the pale straw-coloured liquid and she watched the tiny bubbles sparkle to the surface. 'What are you celebrating? Having the deal signed off?'

'Why not?' he said. He sat down alongside her. 'Or maybe just celebrating the beautiful woman in my bed.' Then he handed her a package that screamed Bulgari.

She just looked at it. 'You don't have to buy me things.'

'I wanted to. Open it.'

She removed the lid, gasping when she saw the magnificent diamond bracelet sparkling inside. She just sat there shaking her head.

'Don't you like it?'

'It's beautiful,' she said, her heart breaking. 'I don't deserve this.'

'I think you do,' he said, removing it from the box and fixing it around her wrist, its diamonds dazzling as they played in the light. He picked up his glass and toasted her. 'Here's to you,' he said before taking a deep sip, his eyes not leaving hers.

He wound an arm around her neck and reeled her in, pressing his mouth to hers. Fine wine seasoned with fine man; his taste was on her lips, his musky male scent curling warmly into her senses, creating a mix that melted her from the bones out and left her weak in his arms. And planted a spark of hope in her heart. A kiss like that had to mean *something*, surely? A gift like that *must* mean something.

Just maybe, if he felt something for her, they might find a way through the mess she'd created.

'You don't like the wine?' he asked when he'd released her and moved to top up his own glass.

She contemplated her flute solemnly and stumbled over her next breath. The moment had finally come. 'Maverick,' she said, 'I need to tell you something.'

His eyebrows lifted and she caught a fleeting shadow skate across his eyes. 'That sounds ominous,' he said as he returned the bottle to the ice bucket without re-filling his glass. 'What's on your mind?'

'There's a couple of things,' she began uncertainly, damning herself for her inability to come right out and say it—*I'm pregnant!*—and be done with it. But her mouth refused to form the words. Instead she had to find out what if anything she meant to him, before she sprung the surprise news that not only was she having his baby but she'd been living a lie these past weeks. She was probably just prolonging her torture, but if she learnt that he had felt something for her during their time together it would be something to cherish in her heart for ever.

'When we started this…' she searched for the right word '…*liaison*, you said it would burn out. Two or three weeks maximum, you said.'

He shrugged. 'You're complaining because we're good together?'

'No. I like the way we, er, *fit*.' She could feel the heat in her face building up, but there was no choice now but to press on. 'But I just don't understand what's going on.'

He leaned over and lifted her chin, pressing his lips to hers, all the while his eyes regarding her coolly. 'What's to understand? We're having an affair. And we're having great sex. Why should there be any more to it than that? Why complicate things?'

She shook her head sadly as his cold words snuffed out the tiny flame of hope she'd nurtured during their day of passion. 'No. No reason,' she agreed, with what she hoped was a smile. It was just as he'd told her it would be. He still expected this thing between them to burn out, and then he'd go back to acting as if it had never happened. It was just taking longer to burn out than he'd expected. 'I was just surprised it had lasted this long. You seemed so sure.'

'I'm as surprised as you are. But why knock it?'

She bit her lower lip. 'What happened with that other person, the one who let you down? What did she do to you that was so bad?'

'Her?' He shook his head. 'Don't give her another thought. She was a bitch. She lied to me. She got pregnant, and—'

His mobile rang out alongside the bed, cutting off his words, and Maverick took one look at the caller ID and stopped. 'Hold on, this is Nell.'

Tegan nodded blindly, too busy concentrating on what he'd said before the interruption to care.

She'd got pregnant.

She'd lied to him.

Those were the sins that had damned the woman. And those were the very same sins of which Tegan herself was guilty. Her heart plummeted to new depths.

There was no hope now.

CHAPTER TEN

SHE sidled out of bed to retrieve her clothes. She'd get dressed and be ready when Maverick finished his call to tell him straight, to tell him the simple truth she should have managed to spit out before now.

'You've been away!' barked his gran's outraged voice.

'To Italy, yes,' he replied, leaning with one elbow against the window frame and gazing out into the night, feeling guilty that he hadn't visited her today on his return. Hadn't given it a thought. 'I told you I was going before I left.'

'Well, that doesn't matter now,' she reasoned, as if she didn't believe him for a minute. 'What does matter is I've sorted out the Christmas problem!'

Maverick sighed. If she banged on again about his parents coming for lunch, he was likely to put his fist through something, most likely the window.

'So, what have you got in mind?'

'And I don't know why you didn't think of it yourself. Or maybe you did, and you were keeping it for a surprise? That would be nice. I like surprises.'

'What are you talking about?' he said, rubbing his brow, rapidly losing patience.

'Vanessa. We'll ask that lovely Vanessa. She'll come to lunch. She'd love to.'

He squeezed his eyes shut, pinching the bridge of his nose. 'You don't think she might already have plans?' He turned around, surprised to see her fully dressed and reaching for her sandals. He frowned. What was that all about? He'd expected she'd stay the night.

'You haven't asked her already, then? I told you you should have thought of it yourself.'

'Gran, she's my PA.'

Tegan looked up at him then, sandals in her hand, a question in her eyes, and he shrugged.

'And that means she doesn't celebrate Christmas? What codswallop!' Nell continued. 'Besides, I've seen the way you look at her, like a rutting elk. It's high time you settled down. You'd be mad to let this one slip through your fingers.'

He had to hand it to Nell, she sure had a fertile imagination. But maybe she had a point. Morgan would be a good distraction on the big day, and maybe it would even cheer her up. She seemed a bit tense about something.

'Okay, Gran,' he soothed. 'But I've got a better idea. We've got a big lunch planned for Christmas Eve with the Royalty Cove team. It'll be a real party—you'll love it. And I know Vanessa's going to be there—yes, I'll make sure of it.' He promised he'd call by tomorrow, then snapped his phone closed and looked over at Morgan. She looked worried about something, no doubt wondering what Nell had been on about.

She took a shaky step closer. 'Maverick, I have to—'

'This Christmas Eve lunch with the Royalty Cove team—you are coming to that?'

She blinked. 'Pardon?'

'Christmas Eve. Nell wants a real Christmas lunch this year, so this is the best solution, so long as you're there. She probably won't even realise it's not Christmas Day. She'll just have a ball.'

Her head shook slowly from side to side. 'I don't think…'

'You'd be doing Nell a huge favour. She's been worried lately about my parents being missing from Christmas. Your presence will be a welcome distraction.'

She screwed up her face, turned it ceilingwards. 'You can't keep doing this!'

'Doing what? Nell likes you. And you'll be at the lunch anyway.' He raised a hand to her shoulder and pulled her close. 'And I wouldn't mind you being there too, if that makes a difference.' ‑

Yes, you would, she thought, given his previous speech about how little she meant to him—and how he sure as hell wouldn't want her there when she revealed the truth.

She shook her head. 'I don't know if I can make it.'

'Of course you will. It's a work function.'

'Christmas Eve is on a Saturday! I don't have to be there.'

'I want you there. And so does Nell. And I warn you, she won't give up. She doesn't find it easy taking no for an answer.'

'It obviously runs in the family,' she snapped, while all the time she was thinking, *Oh God, am I ever going to be able to come clean?* Were her plans always to end in disarray and get her deeper and deeper into this quagmire?

'Making my grandmother happy means a lot to me,' he added.

And her sanity didn't?

She huffed in a breath. 'Okay,' she said, but still shaking her head—knowing she'd regret it, knowing it was only putting off the inevitable, knowing it could only make things so much worse, but unable and unwilling to turn the invitation down. 'I'll come.'

It wasn't all bad news. Two more weeks she got to live the life she'd have chosen if given the choice. Fourteen more days and nights she'd get to spend with Maverick as his mistress, being wined and dined like someone special, like she mattered.

As a child she'd counted down the days before Christmas with relish, marking each and every one off the calendar with boundless excitement and anticipation. This year she scratched the days off the calendar of her heart with dread, as the relentless passage of time brought her closer and closer to the end.

When Morgan finally returned home the day before Christmas Eve, it was hard not to be excited even though she knew it was the final stroke and that there could be no more delays. Tomorrow after the Royalty Cove lunch she would tell Maverick. It wouldn't be much of a Christmas for him—for *either* of them—but at least his grandmother would have her Christmas lunch and at last the air would be cleared.

Morgan was wheeled off the plane in a wheelchair and the sisters greeted each other with tears, one with relief to be home, one with what she was about to lose, but both with love for each other.

Watching the pain twist her twin's face as she manoeuvred her battle-scarred leg into and out of the car was too much for Tegan.

'I thought you were supposed to be better,' Tegan said as she carried her sister's baggage into the apartment. 'I know the office doesn't reopen until New Year's, but do you think you'll be fit enough to resume work by then?'

Morgan smiled wanly, looking weary from the flight, as she gave up the battle with crutches and flopped onto the living room sofa. 'I was going to talk to you about that.'

A new wave of panic skittered down Tegan's spine. 'What do you mean? I thought once you came back you were going to take over your job again.'

'I was hoping to. But the doctors tell me I'll need physio, and weeks of it, before I'm back to normal. I thought about asking you if you could keep filling in…'

Tegan's heart lurched to a standstill before pounding back into life.

'But I thought I'd asked you to do enough. Maybe it's just time I resigned.'

'But you love this job!'

'And you've done your utmost to keep it going for me, I know. But I can't expect you to do any more. I know how you feel about Maverick. You've been desperate to get away.'

Guilt wrapped around Tegan like a shroud. 'Morgan, it's not quite like that. In fact, I guess when it all comes down to it, he's not really that bad.'

Morgan homed in on the comment like a heat-seeking missile. 'He's not that bad? Are we talking about the same Maverick you couldn't wait for me to rescue you from?'

Tegan stalled. 'Oh God, Morgan, I've made such a mess of this! You're going to hate me when you find out what I've done.'

'Why, what have you done? Blown the expense account? Forgotten to pick up Maverick's dry cleaning? What does it matter?'

Tegan just shook her head. 'It's worse,' she said. 'Much worse.'

Morgan wrapped an arm around her sister's back. 'You really are worried. What is it that's happened?'

Tegan dragged in a breath and looked at her sister uncertainly. 'Just that I think I've fallen in love with your boss.'

'With Maverick!' It wasn't really a question. It was a shocked response that told her twin just how unlikely she found the prospect. 'That's impossible. *He's* impossible. How could you?'

Tegan chewed on her cheek. 'I don't know. It just happened. He got under my skin so much, and I irritated the hell out of him, and it just happened. And then we started the affair.'

'What?' Morgan recoiled like she'd just received a shotgun blast. 'You're having an affair—with *my* boss?'

'Guilty,' Tegan said, dropping her head into her hands. 'I didn't want to.'

'Don't tell me,' Morgan interrupted with disbelief. 'It *just happened.*'

'I'm sorry. Why do you think I wanted you to come back so soon? I knew I was in trouble. You were only supposed to have been gone a week.'

'I know, but an affair! With my boss! What were you thinking?'

I was thinking I'd take all I could get, while I could get it.

'It wasn't that simple. Maverick and I rubbed each other up the wrong way. And it was like you said—he was pushy and demanding and unreasonable as any-thing. But he was also as sexy as hell.'

'Fine, but he doesn't date PAs! I told you that.'

'Yeah. Maybe you should have reminded him of that. I sure tried. Look, I'm sorry, sis. I didn't want it to come to this. He said whatever it was between us would burn out, and I thought it would be dead and buried before you came back. But it hasn't, and now I'm set to have a big Christmassy lunch tomorrow with him and his grandmother, and the whole Royalty Cove team. And now you're back and he still thinks I'm you, and I've been lying to everyone and I don't even know who I am any more…'

Tears welled up in her eyes, tears fat with hopeless-ness and anticipated loss and future disasters. Morgan leant over and pulled her into her arms, resting her chin against her twin sister's head.

'Hey, Tiggy, don't worry. I'm sure it will work out somehow. And maybe falling in love and having an affair with him wasn't a great idea, but you just have to look on the bright side.'

'You mean there's a bright side?'

'Yeah,' Morgan assured her, giving her sister a squeeze. 'It could always be worse, silly. At least you're not pregnant.'

Tegan stiffened in the hug and her sister slowly released her enough to look into her eyes, only to do a double take at what she saw there. 'Oh, Tiggy,' she said, pulling her into her arms again. 'Please, no, not that.'

Christmas Eve bloomed bright and beautiful, with a bank of fat white clouds hovering over the hinterland that gave promise of a sticky summer's day to follow.

The sisters sat quietly subdued, Morgan enjoying her first latte for weeks, Tegan sipping gingerly on a cup of weak tea after the eggs and toast her sister had just about had to force feed her. Her stomach had just started to feel unsettled in the mornings, but how much was due to the baby and how much was sheer dread with what lay before her she wasn't sure.

'I think I should come with you,' Morgan said suddenly. 'You can't face Maverick on your own. Not like this.'

'No. I made this mess. I need to sort it out.'

'But I got you involved in the first place. You were only doing me a favour.'

'Hey, you didn't force me to have an affair with your boss, and you sure as hell didn't get me pregnant.'

'But, Tiggy—'

She held up a hand. 'Thanks, but every time I've tried to tell him the truth something has happened, and it's ended up getting more involved. This is something I have to unravel. Besides, you're hardly up to taking on Maverick right now.'

'He'll want to see me eventually. Probably just to sack me. But I need to talk to him too, if only to apologise for everything.'

Tegan squeezed her sister's hand. 'I know. But let me be the one to break the news, okay?'

Morgan nodded. 'You know, maybe it won't be as bad as you think. If he was attracted to you enough to break his mantra never to get involved with his staff, maybe he won't be so upset about a baby.'

'Nice try, but no. I asked him about Tina—about what she'd done that was so bad. He told me himself— she'd got pregnant and she'd lied to him. I don't think he's going to be too happy about another woman committing the same crimes.'

'So what's the plan?'

Tegan took their empty cups to the sink. 'I told Maverick I'd meet him at his house at twelve. I didn't want him coming here.' She glanced over at the wall clock. 'Which gives me two and a half hours to work up a smile. Do you think I'll make it?' It didn't seem anywhere near enough time, given it felt more like she was heading for the executioner than to a Christmas lunch.

Maverick stashed the shop-wrapped presents on the back seat and eased into the driver's seat, feeling good as he set the powerful Mercedes into action. For the first time in what seemed like for ever he felt good about Christmas. For the first time in years he was actually looking forward to lunch with Nell.

He had to hand it to her, though: for someone who could be so frustrating, she sure had some good ideas from time to time. It wasn't Christmas Day, but lunch with Nell today with Morgan wouldn't be half the ordeal it usually was.

The warming air curled from his open window through his hair, just like anticipation curled in his gut. He was already looking forward to seeing her. But then he was getting used to having Morgan around. Very used to it. Yet a few weeks ago he never would have believed it possible—that he might have an affair with a member of his staff, and a long one, at least by his standards. Even more surprisingly, he was in no hurry to end it. He was enjoying having her around too much.

So much so that when she'd insisted on spending last

night back at her place to check everything was all right, and to catch up with her sister, he'd almost insisted he come with her—and not only to see if she was just using this mysterious sister as an excuse once again. And he'd missed her more than he'd expected last night. He'd reached out his arm and felt nothing, and had missed her sweet curves and satiny skin and the press of her warm body against his. For the first time in a lot of mornings, he'd woken up without the scent of her perfume flavouring his bed, and he hadn't liked it one bit.

So he was in no mood to wait until twelve. Besides, it made no sense for her to drive over to his place when both the nursing home and the restaurant were in the other direction.

Picking her up was a much better idea. He allowed himself a smile. And, if they had a bit of time to kill before they had to pick up Nell, so much the better.

He pulled up alongside the row of townhouses and headed up the path to her door.

He could hardly wait.

There was no answer straight away, and it occurred to him that he should have called her first to let her know he was coming, but then the door swung open. 'Happy Christmas, Morgan,' he said, holding out a small, brightly wrapped gift.

Her look of shock brought him up first, closely followed by the realisation that she was currently propped up on crutches with one leg curled up beneath her.

'What happened to you?' He started. 'Why didn't you call?'

Behind her there was movement, and someone flashed into view in a dressing gown with a towel around her hair. And that one was Morgan too, only more so if it were possible—and suddenly there were two of them, looking at him like rabbits caught in a spotlight, and despite the warm summer day the atmosphere inside the apartment suddenly seemed tight and needle sharp. Something in his gut clamped down tight. That Morgan had a sister was no surprise, but *this*? Something here was very wrong.

The one at the door on crutches turned to the other and said, 'Oh, Tiggy, I had no idea. I'm so sorry.'

CHAPTER ELEVEN

'WHAT the hell's going on?' he demanded, and Tegan wanted to shrink away and disappear into the woodwork. She was so not ready for this. Except that would leave Morgan facing him at the door, and her twin was even less prepared.

She stepped forward. 'Maverick, this is my fault.'

'No,' her sister insisted at the door. 'It's all my fault.'

'What's all your fault?' Maverick demanded, stepping over the threshold past her into the apartment.

'Everything,' both women said in unison.

He didn't understand how there could be two of them, but he knew without thinking that the one in the robe was the one he'd come here to see.

'Morgan, what the hell's going on?'

Her large hazel eyes opened even wider, their green hints flaring up with what looked like pure panic as she pulled the dressing gown tighter around her. The one behind him started to say something, but Morgan stopped her with just a look before returning her eyes to his. 'That's just it,' she said with a hint of resignation. 'I'm not Morgan.'

'What do you expect me to call you?' he growled. '*Vanessa?*'

Slowly she shook her head. 'No. I was going to tell you today, after lunch, but my name is actually Tegan.' She pointed at the woman who was slowly shifting herself from the door, and now stood to one side, resting on her crutches. '*That's* Morgan.'

He swung around. 'What the hell have you two been playing at?'

Guilt was written all over Morgan's stricken features. 'I'm sorry. We swapped places. Tiggy—*Tegan*—pretended to be me. It was only supposed to be for a week.'

'And you both thought you'd get away with that?'

'You weren't supposed to be there. I thought it would be okay. You were supposed to be in Milan. And then I had an accident and was laid up in hospital and couldn't get back.'

He thought back. *That* week! The week he'd come in and found his PA slicking those next-to-nothing stockings up her legs. No wonder she'd looked so shocked. *No wonder she'd seemed so different.*

She'd looked the same, more or less. She'd worked more or less the same, tripping over the occasional name or contact, but she'd been a different person entirely.

'And you thought it was perfectly acceptable to get your twin to stand in for you?'

She swallowed. 'I didn't want to, but I had no other choice. Tegan agreed to fill in for me to look after my job—'

'*What* job?' he roared. 'Do you honestly think you've got a job any more? You must be out of your mind.'

The woman he'd thought of for the past seven weeks as Morgan, only to discover now that she wasn't, bowled forward and wrapped an arm around her sister's shoulders. 'There's no need to yell! Can't you see she's hurt?'

'And you,' he said, 'should stay out of this.'

'Why?' she demanded. 'Yes, it was Morgan's job, but I'm the one who agreed to pretend to be her for a week. So get stuck into me, not her.'

'You should have told me that first day.'

'Don't you think I wanted to? Do you think I enjoyed putting up with you? I wanted so badly to tell you where to shove your job, but I couldn't. For Morgan's sake, I couldn't.'

'For Morgan's sake. What about the *job's* sake? Did you ever spare that a thought?'

'I did the work. And I did it well, you can't deny that, can you?'

'While all the time,' he argued, preferring to let that question slip conveniently aside, 'you were pretending to be someone else.'

'And yet if you'd agreed to Morgan's request for one week's leave—one lousy week's leave, while you weren't even supposed to be there—to enable her to go to her best friend's wedding like she wanted, then I wouldn't have had to stand in for her, and *none* of this would have happened!'

'It wasn't convenient.'

'What—not convenient to you? And that's all that matters? Forget that she's going to miss her best friend's wedding?'

Damn her! He wasn't going to be made to feel like he'd done wrong in this. 'That doesn't matter. Because I *was* there that week, and you *did* pretend to be her, and it *has* happened.'

'And aren't I damned well living with the consequences!'

He looked at the two of them standing alongside each other, identical features, yet one pale and worried and the other with her colour up, eyes wild and her breathing pumping. He wondered why the difference between the two hadn't hit him before. Morgan was…well, she was Morgan. The same as she'd ever been in the eighteen months she'd worked for him—meek and mild and restrained. Whereas Tegan had been full-on from the day she'd arrived in the office.

He should have picked it.

He prided himself on being savvy. So why hadn't he realised she wasn't who she said she was?

Why hadn't he stuck to his vow never to get involved with the staff?

The answer hit him like a blow to the gut.

From the moment he'd seen those legs pointing skywards, he hadn't cared enough about the differences, and he'd been prepared to overlook the fact she was his PA—he'd simply been way too occupied about how he'd been going to get her into his bed.

Before he could respond, Tegan's arm withdrew from her sister's shoulders. She clamped the other hand over her mouth, and with a muffled cry bolted from the room. He looked at Morgan. 'What's wrong with her?'

The remaining woman looked sideways at him. 'Maybe you should ask her that yourself.'

The noise in his ears grew to a roar. The colour he saw when he closed his eyes was red—blood red. The colour of fury. *The colour of deception.*

It was Tina all over again, she of the French-polished talons and cunning mind, who'd cold-heartedly planned both her marriage and her abortion with the same meticulous eye for detail. Ambitious Tina, who'd used an inconvenient pregnancy and an error in judgement on his part as a way out of her nine-to-five life and a meal ticket for life.

And he'd sworn it would never happen again!

'Morgan!' he yelled after her, realising too late but beyond caring that he'd called the wrong name, following the sounds of her distress to what had to be the bathroom, testing the handle and finding it locked, banging on the door. 'What the hell is going on?'

It seemed like for ever before finally he heard the lock being released and the door opened slowly. All her colour was gone, her features suddenly pale and tight.

'So you're pregnant,' he snarled, hoping for a denial, fearing there would be none.

She flicked her eyes up at him, the fight in them long gone before she flattened herself against the wall, and she slid unsteadily past him in the direction of the living room. 'I was going to tell you that today as well.'

'Of course you were. I can hear it now. "Happy Christmas, Maverick. Hey, guess what? I've been impersonating your PA for two months. Oh, and, by the way, I'm pregnant".'

'Yeah, well, it always promised to be a big day.' She looked around but the living room was empty. Morgan had obviously taken refuge in her room and wouldn't have to be party to the revelations and fallout, part two. *Smart move.*

He grabbed her by the upper arm and pulled her around to face him. 'You think this is funny? Because I sure as hell don't.'

'And I thought it was such a scream. Or maybe it's

just throwing up that puts me in such a fun mood.' She glared down at the hand circling her arm. 'And now, if you'd kindly unhand me?'

He let her go with a snort, wheeling away and striding around the living room, shrinking it to a fraction of its size and filling the space with his darkthundercloud presence.

She rubbed the place he'd held her as she watched him pace. He hadn't hurt her, but that old familiar burn was there, like he'd branded her skin with just his touch and left it heated and craving still more. Then he jerked to a stop in that gunslinger stance she'd come to know so well, pointing his finger at her like he was set to fire off a gun.

'What the hell led you to believe you'd get away with this?'

She hugged both arms and shook her head. There was no point wanting him now. No point craving his touch.

Because she'd lied to him.

Because she was pregnant.

And he'd found out about both in the worst possible way.

She was damned.

Would he understand if she tried to explain? She hardly understood it herself. But the least he deserved was an explanation.

'It wasn't about getting away with it. Rather, just a case of trying to get through it with the least possible damage to everyone. And I *was* going to tell you today. After lunch with Nell. I've actually tried to tell you a few times now, but every time I've tried something else has happened to get in the way.'

'How convenient!'

'Frustrating, more like it.'

He shot her a glance that told her he didn't believe a word she said. 'I bet.'

'Okay, if it makes you feel better, I found a way to justify any delay in telling you every time. I convinced myself that I was doing the right thing, and maybe I wasn't. But do you think I enjoyed lying to everyone—having everyone believing I was my sister? No. It was supposed to be for one week, when you wouldn't even be there. Instead it's turned into my own personal hell. But, damn it, I did try to tell you, and every single time something happened that meant that I couldn't.'

'Like when?'

'Like the Monday morning, just after that first time…' She lifted her eyes, caught the spasm in his jaw. 'I'd left you Saturday to go and pick up Morgan from the airport, hoping she might somehow forgive me for sleeping with her boss, and no doubt ruining the job she'd asked me to babysit—only to find a message that she'd been involved in an accident and wouldn't be back for weeks. I knew it was wrong to keep pretending. And I couldn't do it, especially not after what had happened between us. So when I went into the office that next Monday I was intending to tell you the truth.'

'But you said nothing!'

'I started to! But then you sprang the news that Phil Rogerson wanted me as part of the design team, and before I knew it we were headed out to his office and he told me that he felt I was someone he could trust. How do you think I felt? How could I say anything then? All I could do was make sure I did the best job I could.'

'And that's it?'

'No. Then you talked me into an affair that was going to burn out in two weeks. Two weeks!' She laughed, the idea so crazy in retrospect. 'And I was so tempted. Because I knew I could do the job—you believed I was Morgan, and she wouldn't be back until long after our "two-week fling" was over. So I convinced myself it could work.' She paused, and held out her hands.

'But it didn't burn out, and instead I let myself get more deeply involved, with the work and with you.' She swallowed, hoping she was making sense as Maverick's stone-cold gaze flicked over her, his silence every bit as damning as his harsh words of earlier.

It was no doubt pointless, but she had no option other than to plough on. 'And when every attempt I made to tell you backfired,' she whispered, 'I wasn't really sorry at all—and yet I knew that the longer my masquerade continued the worse it had to get. Then I found out I was pregnant...'

'So who's the unlucky man?'

Shock exploded like a bomb blast inside her, horror following in its wake.

'You can't mean that,' she whispered, her whole body trembling, her voice quaking as instinctively she placed a hand low over her belly to protect her unborn child from its father's cruel words. 'I can't believe you even have the audacity to ask.'

He made a sound like a low laugh. 'With your track record, what do you expect?'

'We've been having an affair for something like six weeks now, and still you have to ask me how I happen to be pregnant? Can't you work it out? There's been no one else, before or during this relationship. This is *your* baby, Maverick. Your baby growing inside me. And, heaven help the poor child, but it's yours whether you believe it or not.'

'I used protection!'

'Which obviously failed to protect!'

His jaw was set like stone, his eyes glittering like dark stars.

'How long have you known?'

'I found out when you were in Milan,' she admitted softly, her nerves tangled and snarled like plant roots wound tightly around the confines of a too-small pot.

'You've known for two weeks?'

She flinched at the harshness of his tone, only managing a nod in response.

'And, even when you discovered you were carrying what you say is my child, you chose to keep me in the dark.'

'It is your child!'

'That you obviously decided I didn't need to know about.'

'No,' she conceded. 'As its father you have every right to know.'

'A right that you were more than happy to deny me!'

'I *was* going to tell you. *Today!*'

He shook his head. 'If I hadn't turned up today I'd still be in the dark. And you'd still be lying and pretending.'

She dragged in air, her gut churning anew, her brain churning in sympathy. 'Look, I did try to tell you about the baby—that day I picked you up from the airport— but Nell phoned, and the next thing I know you expect me to be at this lunch today.'

'You could have said no and kept on talking.'

'I didn't want to come! I told you that. But you

insisted, because I was part of the team, because Nell wanted me there. So I put it off. For Nell.'

'For Nell,' he repeated, his words as deadpan as his eyes. 'You apparently do things for other people all the time. You do things for your sister—you lied for her. You were forced to maintain the deception—for Rogerson. You neglected to tell me you're pregnant in deference to Nell's wishes for Christmas. You're a very noble person, it seems. Or is it that you just like to blame everyone else for the bad decisions you make? To see if you can make circumstances work out better for you?'

'Stop twisting things! I was going to tell you! I tried to tell you, but it was *you* who insisted I come to lunch today because Nell was expecting me to be there. That's the *only* reason I agreed.'

'Is it? Are you absolutely sure there isn't another reason you decided to hold back?'

She pulled back, stunned by his certainty, terrified of the implications. Surely he couldn't know! If he had any idea that she loved him, that the promise of living as his mistress for just two more weeks had been too great a temptation for her to resist, then she would not have a shred of pride left to add to her already non-existent self-respect.

'What do you mean?'

'I think that when you heard about this lunch you dreamed up a much more creative way of exploiting the news.'

Cold fingernails scraped down her spine. 'I have no idea what you're talking about.'

'No? So you weren't planning on dropping news of your little secret into the lunch conversation, then?'

She frowned and shook her head. 'With everyone there? Of course not. I told you, I was going to tell you afterwards. Why would I do anything else?'

'Because it's Christmas,' he stated, ignoring her protests. 'And I think you saw the perfect trap. You figured that if you announced your pregnancy during lunch, with everyone including my grandmother in attendance, that I'd be forced into doing the honourable thing and marry you to keep her and everyone else happy.'

'What? That's crazy!'

'Then why wait to tell me until now—when it presents a perfect opportunity to shame me into marriage in front of everyone?'

'And you think you're such a prize? No, thank you. I'm quite capable of taking care of myself and *my* baby.'

'And if it is my baby as well, as you claim?'

'It doesn't matter. You've made it more than plain that you've no interest in this child, which suits me just fine. You've been informed. I've discharged my responsibilities. So now you can forget I ever told you. It's no skin off my nose.'

'And how am I expected to just forget an accusation of paternity now?'

'The same way you quite easily seem able to write off all the good work I have done for your business while I was doing Morgan's job.'

'Not to mention all the good work you performed on your back!'

Icy claws shredded what was left of her heart. 'I can't believe you're saying these things. Haven't you learnt anything at all about me during these last few weeks?'

'Yes,' he said coldly. 'I've learned you're a consummate liar. I've learned you're someone not to be trusted, someone who can twist circumstances to what she'd like them to be.'

She reeled back, stunned by the extent of his hostility. She'd been expecting his censure, she'd been expecting his outrage that she'd deceived him for so long, but she'd never expected his total vilification of her character.

Tegan felt the churning in her stomach take a turn for the worse. 'Oh God,' she muttered, putting one hand over her belly and the back of the other to her mouth, feeling as if she was about to violently lose the next-to-non-existent contents of her stomach once again. It was hardly sympathy she got from him.

'Go and do what you have to do,' he demanded coldly. 'Then get dressed. I'll wait in the car for you. But let me warn you now, don't you dare say a word to anyone!'

Tegan shook her head, not believing, not wanting to believe. 'You've got to be kidding. There's no way… You can't expect me to go. Not now…'

'Just get dressed!' he ordered. 'You don't get out of lunch with my grandmother that easily.'

The restaurant was fully booked, but their table was set in a private room fringed by tall potted-palms, and overlooking a sparkling blue infinity-pool that merged into the sea and azure sky beyond. It was like the Pacific Ocean began and ended at their feet. It was the sort of place that would make you feel good just being there— that is, if you weren't seated next to the Grinch.

'Isn't this nice?' Nell insisted as she took a sip of her

champagne cocktail, oblivious to both her party hat slipping sideways and the simmering tension between two of her lunch companions. 'I haven't had so much fun for ages.'

Tegan smiled thinly and sipped her water, just wanting the ordeal to be over so she could go home and be with her sister. They both had plans to make. Morgan had rehabilitation to organize, and ultimately the search for a new job. Tegan had different plans, plans that included being a single mum and somehow raising a child she felt nowhere near prepared for.

She'd bluffed her way past Maverick's claims, telling him she neither wanted nor needed his help. But she knew her savings wouldn't last for ever, and, while Morgan would be happy to let her stay as long as she needed, she really needed to find a more permanent arrangement before the baby arrived. A single mother. Never in her life had she imagined that would be her fate. Never in her life had she felt so in need of a plan.

But plans and home-making would have to wait. There was still pudding to come, coffee and port, the mere idea of which threatened to turn her stomach again. But nobody else in the party seemed in any mood to hurry things along. It had been a successful year, and with the go-ahead for Royalty Cove the future looked even brighter. Everyone bar Tegan seemed set to celebrate.

She tried to participate in the party mood, and for a while she chatted, but right now the conversation around her blurred into so much white noise as she looked longingly at the sparkling water. She could be floating weightless out there, with not a care in the world, the cool water at her back, the sun warming her face. She'd just drift away, letting the water carry her along, out over the edge of the pool and away into the endless sea, floating away on the gentle waves to where nothing mattered—not an unplanned pregnancy, not the guilt of weeks of deception and not the fact she was in love with a man whose regard for her was so low it didn't register.

Had he ever felt anything for her? She'd thought he had. She'd imagined he must care when he'd cradled her against his warm body at night. If he had once, she'd snuffed out all hope of that today.

She'd let him down. She'd lied to him for the best part of two months, pretending to be someone she wasn't. And then, to top it all off, he'd discovered she was pregnant in the worst possible way.

Was it any surprise he'd called her a consummate liar? Was it any surprise he had doubts that it was even his? Could she really blame him?

'Nell asked you a question.' She looked around to see Maverick staring at her, his features hostile, his eyes carrying a warning for her not to say too much. She knew he still expected her to make some kind of announcement about her pregnancy, and he had planned to seat her half a table away where she couldn't whisper in Nell's ear. But Nell had put paid to that the moment they'd arrived, grabbing hold of Tegan's hand and telling her that she was sitting next to her. Maverick had insisted on sitting alongside her, as if guarding her.

'Sorry, Nell,' she apologised, back to reality. There would be no floating away with this man beside her. Maverick would happily see to it that she sank. 'What was it?'

'I asked what you wanted for Christmas.'

In spite of herself she couldn't help but smile. Nell was so child-like in her delight of Christmas and all the trimmings that went with it. She'd tugged hard on at least half a dozen Christmas crackers, and had laughed wildly at all the jokes. Maybe Tegan should take a leaf out of her book and stop feeling so miserable. At least until lunch was over. It wouldn't have been such an effort, though, if her stomach didn't seem to feel so permanently queasy.

'I'm not expecting anything special,' she said. *Not now*, she thought, with more than a tinge of regret for how Christmas might have been if things had been different, and had she not made such a botched job of letting Maverick discover the truth. But then she was kidding herself. He'd never been going to take the news well, no matter how gently she'd informed him of her deception and the baby. Weeks of pretending to be someone she wasn't, topped off with an unplanned pregnancy—it wasn't the kind of news any man was likely to take kindly to.

Nell patted her hand, the touch of her leathery skin strangely soothing. 'I just bet Santa's got something special in his sack for you.'

Tegan smiled and nodded, but she knew that what she wanted for Christmas, she would never get. Maverick had snuffed out any faint hope that he might forgive her duplicity. There was no way he would ever want her love, let alone reciprocate.

'I know what you need,' Nell continued. 'One of these lovely champagne thingies. Someone pass the wine. Vanessa's glass is empty.'

Phil Rogerson cocked a quizzical eyebrow in her direction as he took a bottle of sparkling wine and topped up Nell's glass before turning to Tegan's. 'No thanks,' she said, covering her glass. 'I'd rather not.' Not when the thought of drinking anything with bubbles, be it alcohol or soft drink, filled her with dread. She didn't need anything else fizzing in her stomach right now.

Phil shrugged and moved on to the next glass. Nell was suddenly watching her like a hawk, and Tegan used the excuse of reaching for her handbag to turn away and hide her face for a few moments, certain her colour was up. She should have let him fill her glass. She didn't have to drink it, after all. At least this might provide a diversion.

She retrieved the small gift she had luckily remembered to bring in all the excitement. 'I was saving this to give you when Christmas pudding arrived, but maybe you should open it now. It's just something small, but I hope you like it.' She held out the small package in the palm of her hand. 'Merry Christmas, Nell.'

'Oh, I love presents!' said Nell, clapping her hands gleefully, an undisguised glint of joy in her eyes. 'What is it?'

Tegan smiled. 'Open it and see.'

Nell ripped off the paper like a six-year-old, and opened the small box with such a look of anticipation that Tegan couldn't help but feel good, no matter what the man at her side thought of her.

'Oh, it's beautiful!' Nell cried. 'Look, Maverick, look what Vanessa's given me.' Her gnarled fingers did battle to manoeuvre out the antique cameo-brooch from the box then undo the pin.

'Here,' said Maverick. 'Let me.' He took the brooch and pinned it to Nell's neckline, where she'd indicated.

'It's over one-hundred years old,' Tegan told her, delighted her find from an estate jewellers had been so well received.

'Heavens! It's almost as old as I am!' Nell exclaimed, setting the whole table erupting in laughter as she patted it with one hand, taking Tegan's in her other. 'I love it. You're such a lovely girl. Isn't she a lovely girl, Maverick?'

Maverick grunted his reply, relieved from having to give a more comprehensive answer by the arrival of dessert and Nell's cries of delight.

Tegan had barely touched her dessert before she excused herself from the table, sending his hackles up. She'd toyed with the seafood entrée and the main course as well, chasing food around her plate but hardly catching anything more than morsels. Even her water sat untouched. That was no way to nurture a baby.

Especially not his.

Something ferocious twisted in his gut. Could it be? Was she really carrying his child? He'd promised himself after the Tina debacle that never again would he be put in a situation where he was at the mercy of a woman claiming to be carrying his child. And, when he'd first discovered the news this morning, it had been that bitter past first and foremost in his mind, driving his reaction in a rush of bad blood and acrid memories.

But Tina had never been carrying his baby, and even when he'd believed she had he'd never encountered the curious burst of pride he felt right now.

The thought that she was carrying his child...

God, but it did things to him. It foamed his blood to white hot. It swelled his heart with pride. It made him want to damn her, and yet protect her at the same time. It made him want to howl at the moon and tear someone to pieces…

'Your mother was like that with you, you know. Couldn't bear to touch a drop.'

Gears shifted and crunched in his mind as Nell's words filtered through. 'What are you talking about?'

'Vanessa. Not drinking. Your mother was like that with you. Not like me. Strong as a bear, I was. Never knew a day's morning sickness… Maverick, where are you going?'

CHAPTER TWELVE

SHE patted her face with a damp towel and breathed deeply. She hadn't been ill, but it had been touch and go there for a while. *Morning sickness.* It had to have been a man who'd coined that expression and got it so wrong.

She tossed the hand-towel into the basket on her way out. If she didn't get back soon, guard-dog Maverick would probably put out an APB on her. But outside it was Phil Rogerson she bumped into coming the other way.

'Having a nice lunch?' he asked, smiling broadly.

She smiled and nodded, expecting the exchange to end there and for them to go their separate ways.

'Oh, I meant to ask you,' he added, when he was almost past her. 'Why is it that Nell calls you Vanessa?'

She smiled, not for the first time appreciating the irony. 'She didn't think I looked like a Morgan.'

His head tilted. 'How odd. Well, she's definitely a character.'

Tegan had a quick glance around, saw they were alone and took a fortifying breath. There was no time like the present.

'Actually, Phil,' she started tentatively, 'I've got something I need to tell you. Do you have a moment?'

His brow creased into the time-worn lines that criss-crossed his brow. 'Of course, my dear.' He pointed to a small sitting area on the terrace just outside the restaurant. 'Let's sit there and you can tell me what's on your mind.'

'And that's how it all came about.' Tegan hesitated, trying to gauge his reaction. 'I'm sorry to have deceived you, Phil. I hated doing it, but at the time I couldn't see a way out of it. But I had to tell you myself, before you found out some other way.'

He patted her on the shoulder. 'Well, if it's any consolation, I knew something wasn't quite right. You knew far too much about Sam and what he was doing in Somalia to have just been relaying it from your sister's experiences—but I couldn't put my finger on how it was possible. But now that you've explained your sister is a twin...' He nodded. 'It all falls into place. So, what happens to you now then, now that your secret is out?'

'I don't know, to be honest. I know I've let everyone down. I've got a lot of ground to make up.'

'Well,' he said, patting her hands, 'if you're ever looking for a job, you come and see me. I'll have you back on the dream team before you can say Jack Robinson.'

'Thanks so much, Phil. I've been feeling so guilty. I had to explain to you myself.'

He squeezed her shoulder as they stood. 'I appreciate your telling me. And I think you must be a pretty special sister to not only do what you did, but to carry it off so ably. Hats off to you. And, don't forget, Doris still wants to see your sister—ah!' He corrected himself with a gruff laugh. 'To see *you*, to talk more about what Sam was up to, whenever you can. Okay? Oh, and by the way, Sam called yesterday! He's coming home in three months. Doris is over the moon. Talk about the best Christmas ever.'

He gave her a quick peck on the cheek and wished her a happy Christmas before disappearing back the way they'd come. 'The best Christmas ever'. She was happy for Phil and his family. They deserved it. But she was envious too. It was going to be a long time before she enjoyed the best Christmas ever. She stood for a moment at the railing, enjoying the soft summer breeze that carried the freshness of the ocean. It was the calmness she needed in the midst of a day of turmoil, until another stab of pain sliced through her. Damn! She turned to go inside and almost walked into a wall of man.

'What the hell was that little cosy *tête à tête* all about?'

'Maverick? I just wanted to tell Phil—'

'Like you told Nell?'

His eyes were wild, his face filled with fury, a nerve flicking in his jaw.

'Told Nell what?'

'I knew you'd do this. Even when I'd warned you not to say a word, you just couldn't help yourself. You intended this all along!'

'What are you talking about?'

'Nell knows about the baby. And I take it Phil Rogerson knows now, too. Before long the whole of the Gold Coast will know.'

'What? How does she know?'

'Don't give me that! How do you *think* she knows? You told her.'

'I did no such thing.'

'I knew I couldn't trust you, even when I'd warned you. I should never have brought you to this lunch.'

'For once you've got it right! You shouldn't have brought me here. I didn't want to come, so you can blame yourself. But get one thing straight—I *didn't* tell Nell!'

'Then how does she know?'

Tegan threw a wild shrug into the air and spun around. 'I don't know! Maybe she just made a wild stab in the dark because I wasn't drinking and look like crap. Why don't you ask her instead of accusing me?'

'You don't look that bad.'

'God knows, I feel it.' She shouldn't have spun around. She clamped her hands down on the back of a chair and focused on a spot on the floor, dragging in air while trying to steady herself, praying it and the contents of her stomach wouldn't budge.

'So what did you tell Phil?'

She squeezed closed her eyes. There was an edge to her queasiness that wasn't there before—an intensity that squeezed her gut so sharp and tight it made sweat break out on her brow. Damn him; this was hardly the time to face up to an interrogation!

'I told him that I wasn't really Morgan. I told him I was sorry.'

'And then you told him you were pregnant.'

'*No!* What is your problem? Morgan and you are the only people I've told.'

'This isn't the first time this has happened, you know. I won't be forced into marrying you, no matter how many people you tell.'

'For the last time—*I didn't tell Nell*! I didn't tell Phil. And I am not trying to force you into marrying me.'

'And I don't believe you.'

'You can believe what you like,' she said, already feeling another twist of pain, already determined to get back to the bathroom in the shortest possible time. 'But the simple fact is, right now I wouldn't marry you if you were the last man left on Earth!'

Which suited him just fine. Not that he believed her, or this act she kept putting on every time he went near her. Maybe she hadn't told anyone, but she'd damned sure acted out the part to full effect. He went back to the table to enjoy his coffee and await her return, but the coffee tasted like mud, and then they served Christmas cake and port and still there was no sign of her. Where the hell was she?

He wasn't finished with her yet. She hadn't started paying for the problems she'd caused him. She'd lied to him. She'd pretended to be her sister for seven weeks, and then had tried to justify not telling him every chance she'd got. Now it looked like she'd lied about not telling Nell she was pregnant.

But, damn whatever her name, whoever she was— she'd been *his* woman for all of that time. Seven weeks in his bed, pleasuring him, matching his every need, taking him to places he'd never been.

It galled him to think there were still places he'd like to go and she wouldn't be there.

Like she wasn't here now.

He threw his napkin on the table and found the maître d', only to discover Tegan had ordered a taxi some twenty minutes before.

She'd already left!

His heart froze over in an arctic blast of bitterness. His accusations had been right on target, otherwise why would she have fled the first chance she'd got? She was as guilty as hell.

The party was breaking up. Nell was looking battle-weary, the cameo at her neck taunting him, sticking into his psyche. Damn her! What was this rubbish she'd spouted about not marrying him if he'd been the last man left on Earth? He was the baby's father, not someone she could just write off like that.

He wasn't about to be trapped into anything, but he wasn't about to be written off that easily either!

He'd take Nell home and then he'd go and find Tegan and set her straight.

'I hate him!' Tegan was reclining on the sofa where she'd collapsed the moment she'd got home, her head thrown back, her eyes closed, fingers pinching the bridge of her nose.

Morgan successfully negotiated crutches and boiling water and placed a mug of ginger tea on the table in front of her sister. 'This coming from the woman who told me just last night that she loved him.'

'That was before he accused me of telling the whole world I was pregnant by him.'

'What? Why would he think you would do that?'

'To shame him into marrying me, of course. Seems he really doesn't trust me. Not that I haven't given him good reason, I guess.' She put a hand to her stomach as another cramp seized her. 'Oh God, I feel awful. This can't be normal, surely?'

Morgan looked at her sister, the concern for her twin evident in her eyes. 'Can I get you anything?'

'No, you shouldn't be running after me. I should be taking care of you.'

'Then we'll just have to take care of each other.'

'Thanks, sis. I'm just sorry you had to come home for what has to be the worst Christmas ever.'

'At least I'm home. Anything has to beat being in a hospital miles away for Christmas. And, who knows, maybe things will look brighter tomorrow. Maybe there really is a Santa Claus.'

Tegan tried to smile, but the cramps turned it into a grimace. 'Oh, no, here we go again.' She staggered to her feet to head for the bathroom when the room suddenly tilted and spun as the floor fell away, and then everything turned black.

'Happy Christmas,' said the two old women in chorus as Maverick got out of his car and started up the footpath. He grunted something in response. Christmas wasn't happy from where he was standing. Two ugly mutts on extendable leashes made a rush for him as he passed, but he bared his teeth and growled at them and they wheeled around and fled straight back to their elderly owner, snapping at each other instead.

He strode up the path, reached the front door, pushed the doorbell and waited. Then he pushed it again. And again.

'Are you looking for the Misses Fielding?'

He looked over his shoulder. Both old ladies were peering at him intently. The dogs were sniffing around his car. He pressed the doorbell again, harder this time. 'Just one of them.'

'I'm afraid you've missed all the excitement.'

This time he turned around. 'What excitement?'

'The ambulance. It was a good half-hour ago. Came with lights flashing and siren wailing. I was just telling Deidre Garrett here about it.'

Ambulance? He gave up on the door. 'What happened? Who?'

'That's what we're trying to work out. I never can tell which one is which.'

'Neither can I,' said the one with the dogs. 'I'm always getting them mixed up when they're together. And their names are so confusing too, don't you find?'

He wanted to bellow in frustration. 'Just tell me,' he said, as calmly and emphatically as possible, 'what happened.'

'We're not sure. One of them got wheeled out on the trolley—they had the bag thing set up and everything, tubes going everywhere. And the other one sort of hobbled alongside.'

'Hobbled?'

'Yes, the one that was on crutches. She didn't look much better. They bundled her into the back of the ambulance too, and went off with the siren screaming.'

Tegan!

Something had happened to Tegan.

The baby!

He shouted his thanks as he made a rush for the car, sending dogs scattering. They must have taken her to Gold Coast Central. It was the biggest hospital around, the best emergency department. She had to be there.

She'd left lunch without a word. Oh God, what had he done? He'd even suspected her of faking it.

If anything happened to her he didn't know what he'd do. *Tegan.* And she was having his baby.

Unless…

Is that what had happened—she'd lost their baby? Their child?

Please, God, no. Already he felt like he'd been gutted, his organs hung out to dry.

Nothing must happen to her or the baby. He wouldn't let it. Not before he had a chance to see her, to tell her how sorry he was for all the harsh words he'd spoken, all the things he should have said.

Tegan.

Please God, let it not be too late!

CHAPTER THIRTEEN

'MORGAN!' Maverick ran down the corridor towards the waiting room. 'What happened?'

Morgan swung herself around, stress lining her features. 'Maverick. I'm surprised to see you here.'

'How is she? Can I see her? I have to talk to her.'

'I'm not sure they'll let you.'

'Is it the baby?'

She shook her head. 'She's got food poisoning. On top of morning sickness. She was so dehydrated, she collapsed on the floor.'

'It's my fault. She hardly ate a thing, and I was so angry with her. It's no wonder she got sick.'

'No, if it's any consolation, I actually think it's my fault. I told her she should have something nourishing for breakfast, so I cooked her eggs. They think that's what did it. It's just lucky that her morning sickness took care of most of it.'

'So then—the baby…?'

'Is okay. The paramedics were fantastic. They were there in no time.'

He collapsed into a chair and put his head in his hands. 'Thank God!'

She tucked her crutches together and sat down alongside him. 'She thought you were angry with her.'

He squeezed his eyes tightly shut, trying to block out the pain of remembering what he'd done, what he'd said. 'I was. Very angry.'

'But you really love her, don't you? I mean, you must, otherwise you wouldn't be here. You wouldn't care.'

Something like a thunderbolt shuddered through him. He opened his eyes and looked at the green-grey linoleum floor. It was the same floor he'd closed his eyes on just a few short seconds ago, but somehow it looked different. Everything looked different. Brighter. Sharper.

Everything *felt* different.

Especially inside him.

He loved Tegan. Loved her with a passion that went beyond mere physical desire. Loved her with a force that couldn't have kept him away from her if it had tried.

Why hadn't he realised? Why had it taken him so long? Why had he cost her so much?

His voice was so shaky when it came, it was a wonder it didn't break. 'I do.'

Just saying the words made it more real. More powerful. 'I do,' he repeated, firmer this time, almost like a vow.

'Then maybe you ought to tell her. She was pretty upset when she came home from lunch today.'

He closed his eyes again, nodding. He could imagine. He'd been relentless in his accusations, relentless in his cruelty.

Beside him Morgan sighed. 'Just don't be surprised if she doesn't want to see you.'

And pain sliced his heart anew.

* * *

'What do you want?'

It was the next morning before they let him in, after Morgan had convinced her to agree to see him. And her first sentence let him know just how low on the register he'd reduced himself to.

He'd spent the night thinking about everything she'd said, replaying all her defences, trying to put together the pieces of the puzzle. She'd been right. She had tried to tell him, or at least talk to him, and he'd cut off her opportunities every time.

He'd known something was up that time he'd returned from Italy and she'd been asking strange questions. She'd told him she wanted to talk. And then Nell had called and things had got messy.

He hadn't let her explain. And, in doing so, he'd driven her deeper and deeper into her duplicity.

He entered the room, feeling more out of control than he'd ever felt in his life. She lay leaning against the pillows in a white hospital gown, her hair swept back from her face, a drip feeding liquids into her arm. Her skin was pale, but her features were set to defiant, her hazel eyes and mouth resolute.

He stopped halfway into the room. 'Tegan...' he started inadequately.

'I had to tell the medical staff I was pregnant,' she snapped. 'I'm sorry if that was against the rules, but don't worry, I swore them all to secrecy.'

He held his breath. He deserved that. He deserved everything she wanted to dish out and more.

'How are you feeling?'

'It's just the best Christmas morning I've ever had. What do you reckon?'

'They tell me the baby is okay.'

'What—so now you care about the baby? That's a turn-up. What did you come here for, Maverick? To have another go at me? To make me feel even worse? Because you know, if Morgan hadn't convinced me to see you, you wouldn't be here at all. So, please, just make it quick.'

'No,' he said, moving closer to the bed. 'I don't want to make you feel worse. I came to make sure you were all right. When I heard you'd been taken to hospital, I just about went crazy. I had to see you. I had to tell you I was sorry.' He took a step closer to the bed. 'And only last night I realised why it mattered.'

'Because you wanted your baby back? Sorry, it's a done deal.'

'No. Because I only realised when I got here why it was so important I see you. Because I love you.'

For a split second she didn't react, and he held out hope that he'd said the words she most wanted to hear. But then she scoffed, holding a hand to her head. 'Is that supposed to be a joke? Because, if you're serious, I have to say you've sure got a funny way of showing it.'

'Tegan, I'm so sorry. For the things I said, for the way I treated you. I'm sorry for everything. I didn't realise you were so sick yesterday. I should never have got stuck into you like that at all, but while you were so sick it was inexcusable.'

'You thought I was faking it, so everyone would know I was pregnant and you'd be forced into marrying me.'

He turned his head away, ashamed because what she'd said was true.

'There is a reason,' he said.

'A reason you treated me like crap?'

'I told you about Tina.'

'The PA who left you so scarred and cynical. She lied to you. She got pregnant. That's what you told me.'

'She did.'

'As did I! I lied to you about who I was. I got pregnant. Obviously I deserved the worst.'

'It's not the same.' He took a deep breath, raked his hands through his hair. 'I thought it was, but it's not. Tina's baby wasn't mine. She got pregnant and decided it was her meal ticket. We were working late one night and she made a move on me. She was from a Greek family, and had very striking looks… And, well, one thing led to another. A few weeks later she told me the baby was mine and that her family would disinherit her. I had no reason not to believe her. So I did the honourable thing—I told her I'd marry her.'

'How did you find out?'

'Just before the wedding. I overheard her boasting about it to a friend, about how she'd sucked me in completely and had already booked the abortion clinic. She was planning to destroy the child she'd used to trap me with as soon as our honeymoon was over.'

'Oh my God. How could she?'

'When I learned you were pregnant, it was Tina happening all over again. I was angry at you, but I was madder at myself for letting it happen. It's not an excuse. I'm not trying to claim that what happened all those years ago excuses my behaviour. But I just want you to understand why I acted the way I did, and why I jumped to the conclusions that I did—the wrong ones, I know now.'

She blinked and just stared at him, and he was brave enough to walk to her side and sit down on her bed. 'I guess it didn't help to have it all dumped on you yesterday like that. I hadn't planned it that way. I did try to tell you before, several times. Honest.'

'I know. I didn't give you a chance to tell me.'

She reached out a hand to his arm. 'You really believe that?'

'I didn't before.' He caught her hand in his, then spread his fingers wide, matching hers palm to palm before wrapping it once more in his. 'I was too blind with anger to see anything. I wasn't thinking. I was reliving the past, and I failed to see you. I only saw Tina and what she'd planned. What she'd done. But I do believe you now. I remembered the times I cut you off. I remembered you asking me not to keep doing this to you. I remembered your frustration. And it all made sense.'

She frowned, and moved to pull her hand away. 'You know, Maverick, I still haven't been completely honest with you.'

He wouldn't let go. 'What's that supposed to mean? It *is* my baby?'

'Yes, of course it's yours. There's been no one else. There *is* no one else. But do you remember when you told me about Tina? You were just back from Milan. I asked you about her because I needed to know where I stood with you—how you felt about me before I told you the truth, because I knew you'd hate me then. And, when I asked you what she'd done to you, you said those two things—that she'd lied to you and she'd got pregnant. And I got scared. I was guilty of the very same sins. So I got out of bed while you were on the phone and got dressed, because I knew you'd throw me out the minute I told you. But then Nell asked that I be at the lunch if she was going, and you insisted, and I told myself that I was doing it for Nell. I told you that in my defence. Nell gave me a gold-plated reason not to tell you.'

'I know. I understand.'

She shook her head. 'But you don't. Because I didn't do it for Nell. Not entirely. You were right when you mocked me. Because I did it for me. I took the option of staying your mistress for two more weeks over being honest with you then. I took the path of least resistance. Oh, I liked Nell, and wanted her to be happy, but *I* wanted to be happy even more. I couldn't bear the thought of losing you, and I knew that if I told you that's exactly what would happen. I knew I was taking a risk, and it couldn't help but end ugly, and it did.'

'I'm sorry I made it so ugly for you.'

'You couldn't help it. I left you no option. I lied to you from the start. I pretended to be someone else. I can't blame you for hating me.'

'You haven't been listening to me. I told you, I love you.'

She shook her head. 'You can't mean that. Not after everything that's happened. You don't have to be nice to me just because it's Christmas. I'm not going to make you marry me like that other woman. You don't have to pretend.'

He allowed himself a smile. 'I'm not being nice to you because it's Christmas. And I know you wouldn't marry me if I was the last man left on Earth, but I was wondering…'

He picked up both her hands in his, stroking the back of them with his thumbs, so tender where the canula was taped into one.

'I was wondering whether you'd consider having

me as your husband if maybe I *wasn't* the last man left on Earth?'

She looked up at him. 'You're asking me to marry you?'

'No,' he said. 'I'm begging you to marry me.'

'Because I'm having your baby?'

'The baby is a bonus. I want to marry you because I love you, and I can't stand the thought of trying to live without you.'

'You *really* love me?'

'With all my heart and soul.'

She threw her arms around his neck. 'Of course I will. I have loved you for so long!'

He put her away by the shoulders. 'You have? Why didn't you tell me?'

'How could I, when I wasn't even me? How could I admit anything? I didn't even know who I was supposed to be. And meanwhile you were expecting this thing between us to burn out in two weeks.'

He looked into her eyes. 'This *thing* between us is never going to burn out—you better believe it.'

She looked up at him, her colour back, her eyes warm and delicious, her lips an open invitation. 'I want to believe it.'

'Then maybe this will convince you,' he said, and lowered his mouth to hers. He kissed her, with all the depths of passion that he felt for her, with all the respect she deserved for what she'd done, with all the love for her that would never be more than she deserved.

And he felt her love in her kiss, in the way her arms pulled him to her, in the way her mouth moved under his.

The door burst open and a nurse bustled in. 'Everything all right in here? This man isn't bothering you, is he, Miss Fielding? Your sister sent me in to check.'

'No,' she said, looking into the eyes of the man she loved, the father of her child, the man she was going to marry. 'He's not bothering me at all. Tell Morgan everything is just perfect. And you know what else you can tell her for me?'

The nurse looked a little perplexed. 'What's that?'

Without taking her eyes from his, she smiled up at him, a smile that he'd been looking for for ever, a smile that he would treasure until the day he died, and his heart swelled like it was about to burst.

'Just tell her there really *is* a Santa Claus.'

EPILOGUE

MAVERICK hated to be kept waiting. He hated not being in control, and he hated feeling helpless. And more than anything he hated watching the woman he loved in so much pain, her brow glistening with perspiration, her face contorted with every contraction. So he was damn sure he never wanted to go through this whole childbirth experience again.

That is until, with one final push, their baby emerged with a short cry into the world.

Their baby.

He squeezed Tegan's hand and watched with awe and frustration while the cord was clamped and cut and the baby assessed.

'Congratulations,' said the midwife, smiling broadly as she handed the wrapped child to its mother. 'You have a beautiful baby girl.'

'Nell was right!' she cried as she cradled the child against her breast. 'We have a daughter.'

She was beautiful, with a shock of black hair that framed her face, a tiny Cupid's bow mouth and muddy blue eyes that looked up at her mother in fascination as she wriggled her limbs, testing her new-found freedom.

Maverick found himself moved to tears. Never had he seen a more perfect picture than the one before him now: the woman he loved holding the baby they'd created together.

His woman.

His child.

His fortune.

'She is beautiful,' he agreed huskily, planting a kiss on their daughter's downy, soft hair before turning to his wife. 'Just like her mother.'

The team quietly and efficiently finished up around them in the minutes following, and drifted away one by one, leaving the new family some time to get acquainted.

Maverick had his turn to cuddle the tiny bundle, letting its hand latch onto his finger, feeling the strength of her grip, and he was totally bewitched. She was so utterly defenceless and yet, like the tiny hand around his finger, already she had a powerful grip around his heart.

'So what do we call you, little one?' he asked.

'Nell knew that too,' Tegan offered. 'She's our Christmas gift. We should call her Holly. Holly Eleanor, after your gran.'

'Holly Eleanor? I like it.' He looked into the peaceful face of his wife, her beautiful face calm now where previously her features had been contorted with pain, her hair waving in curls around her face where before it had been slick with sweat. Never had he had more admiration and respect for a person than he did now.

'You were truly magnificent back there,' he told her. 'I wanted to do something, *anything*, to help you but there was nothing I could do.'

She responded with a dazzling smile that made him feel good all the way down to his toes. 'Just having you here holding my hand was all the help I needed,' she said. 'Thank you.'

'No.' he said. 'Thank you. You saved me. Last Christmas I was nothing more than a cynical business-man—"self-aggrandising"—isn't that how you put it?'

She laughed. 'Oh, my, did I really say that?'

'And you were right. All I cared about was Royalty Cove and making it a success.'

'And you cared about Nell! But Royalty Cove is a great success. Otherwise why would Zeppabanca want to take the concept to Italy?'

'Well, they'll be taking it there without me. I've sug-gested Rogerson head the deal this time.'

'But it's what you wanted. It's what you were working towards all along.'

He shook his head. 'Only because I didn't know what was really worth chasing. I don't need more money, not now I've found you. You've taught me there's something far more precious—your love— love that comes from the heart. And I love you for saving me, Tegan, with all my heart and soul. And today, with your gift of Holly Eleanor, I love you more than ever.'

Her eyes glowed with happiness. 'You're the father of my child. How could I not love you? But then I feel sometimes that I've always loved you, and that I was just waiting to meet you.'

'I'm so glad Morgan decided to go to that wedding,' he murmured, drawing closer. 'Remind me to thank her next time I see her.'

He wound his free arm behind his wife's neck and

pulled her in close for a kiss, their child squirming in protest between them.

Tegan broke the kiss with a laugh. 'What's wrong, little Holly, are we ignoring you?' she asked, placing her own hand under the child alongside Maverick's, and gazing down at the face of her baby. 'You know, I do believe this coming Christmas is going to be even more special than last year's.'

Maverick didn't doubt it. 'With you in my life,' he told her, 'every single day is going to be special.'

And it was.

* * * * *

SPECIAL EDITION

Life, Love and Family

*These contemporary romances will strike a chord
with you as heroines juggle life
and relationships on their way to true love.*

New York Times *bestselling author Linda Lael Miller
brings you a BRAND-NEW contemporary story
featuring her fan-favorite McKettrick family.*

Meg McKettrick is surprised to be reunited with
her high school flame, Brad O'Ballivan. After
enjoying a career as a country-and-western singer,
Brad aches for a home and family…and seeing
Meg again makes him realize he still loves her. But
their pride manages to interfere with love…until
an unexpected matchmaker gets involved.

*Turn the page for a sneak preview of
THE McKETTRICK WAY by Linda Lael Miller
On sale November 20, wherever books are sold.*

Brad shoved the truck into gear and drove to the bottom of the hill, where the road forked. Turn left, and he'd be home in five minutes. Turn right, and he was headed for Indian Rock.

He had no damn business going to Indian Rock.

He had nothing to say to Meg McKettrick, and if he never set eyes on the woman again, it would be two weeks too soon.

He turned right.

He couldn't have said why.

He just drove straight to the Dixie Dog Drive-In.

Back in the day, he and Meg used to meet at the Dixie Dog, by tacit agreement, when either of them had been away. It had been some kind of universe thing, purely intuitive.

Passing familiar landmarks, Brad told himself he ought to turn around. The old days were gone. Things had ended badly between him and Meg anyhow, and she wasn't going to be at the Dixie Dog.

He kept driving.

He rounded a bend, and there was the Dixie Dog. Its big neon sign, a giant hot dog, was all lit up and going through its corny sequence—first it was covered in red squiggles of light, meant to suggest ketchup, and then yellow, for mustard.

Brad pulled into one of the slots next to a speaker, rolled down the truck window and ordered.

A girl roller-skated out with the order about five minutes later.

When she wheeled up to the driver's window, smiling, her eyes went wide with recognition, and she dropped the tray with a clatter.

Silently Brad swore. Damn if he hadn't forgotten he was a famous country singer.

The girl, a skinny thing wearing too much eye makeup, immediately started to cry. "I'm sorry!" she sobbed, squatting to gather up the mess.

"It's okay," Brad answered quietly, leaning to look down at her, catching a glimpse of her plastic name tag. "It's okay, Mandy. No harm done."

"I'll get you another dog and a shake right away, Mr. O'Ballivan!"

"Mandy?"

She stared up at him pitifully, sniffling. Thanks to the copious tears, most of the goop on her eyes had slid south. "Yes?"

"When you go back inside, could you not mention seeing me?"

"But you're Brad O'Ballivan!"

"Yeah," he answered, suppressing a sigh. "I know."

She rolled a little closer. "You wouldn't happen to have a picture you could autograph for me, would you?"

"Not with me," Brad answered.

"You could sign this napkin, though," Mandy said. "It's only got a little chocolate on the corner."

Brad took the paper napkin and her order pen, and scrawled his name. Handed both items back through the window.

She turned and whizzed back toward the side entrance to the Dixie Dog.

Brad waited, marveling that he hadn't considered incidents like this one before he'd decided to come back home. In retrospect, it seemed shortsighted, to say the least, but the truth was, he'd expected to be—Brad O'Ballivan.

Presently Mandy skated back out again, and this time she managed to hold on to the tray.

"I didn't tell a soul!" she whispered. "But Heather and Darlene *both* asked me why my mascara was all smeared." Efficiently she hooked the tray onto the bottom edge of the window.

Brad extended payment, but Mandy shook her head.

"The boss said it's on the house, since I dumped your first order on the ground."

He smiled. "Okay, then. Thanks."

Mandy retreated, and Brad was just reaching for the food when a bright red Blazer whipped into the space beside his. The driver's door sprang open, crashing into the metal speaker, and somebody got out in a hurry.

Something quickened inside Brad.

And in the next moment Meg McKettrick was standing practically on his running board, her blue eyes blazing.

Brad grinned. "I guess you're not over me after all," he said.

REQUEST YOUR FREE BOOKS!

 HARLEQUIN *Presents*

PASSION GUARANTEED SEDUCTION

2 FREE NOVELS PLUS 2 FREE GIFTS!

YES! Please send me 2 FREE Harlequin Presents® novels and my 2 FREE gifts. After receiving them, if I don't wish to receive any more books, I can return the shipping statement marked "cancel." If I don't cancel, I will receive 6 brand-new novels every month and be billed just $3.80 per book in the U.S., or $4.47 per book in Canada, plus 25¢ shipping and handling per book and applicable taxes, if any*. That's a savings of close to 15% off the cover price! I understand that accepting the 2 free books and gifts places me under no obligation to buy anything. I can always return a shipment and cancel at any time. Even if I never buy another book from Harlequin, the two free books and gifts are mine to keep forever.

106 HDN EEXK   306 HDN EEXV

Name	(PLEASE PRINT)

Address	Apt. #

City	State/Prov.	Zip/Postal Code

Signature (if under 18, a parent or guardian must sign)

Mail to the **Harlequin Reader Service**®:
IN U.S.A.: P.O. Box 1867, Buffalo, NY 14240-1867
IN CANADA: P.O. Box 609, Fort Erie, Ontario L2A 5X3

Not valid to current Harlequin Presents subscribers.

Want to try two free books from another line?
Call 1-800-873-8635 or visit www.morefreebooks.com.

* Terms and prices subject to change without notice. NY residents add applicable sales tax. Canadian residents will be charged applicable provincial taxes and GST. This offer is limited to one order per household. All orders subject to approval. Credit or debit balances in a customer's account(s) may be offset by any other outstanding balance owed by or to the customer. Please allow 4 to 6 weeks for delivery.

Your Privacy: Harlequin is committed to protecting your privacy. Our Privacy Policy is available online at www.eHarlequin.com or upon request from the Reader Service. From time to time we make our lists of customers available to reputable firms who may have a product or service of interest to you. If you would prefer we not share your name and address, please check here. ☐

HP07

▼ *Silhouette*®

SPECIAL EDITION™

**brings you a heartwarming
new McKettrick's story from**

NEW YORK TIMES BESTSELLING AUTHOR

LINDA LAEL MILLER

THE McKETTRICK *Way*

Meg McKettrick is surprised to be reunited
with her high school flame, Brad O'Ballivan,
who has returned home to his family's
neighboring ranch. After seeing Meg again,
Brad realizes he still loves her. But the pride
of both manage to interfere with love...until
an unexpected matchmaker gets involved.

—— McKettrick Women ——

Available December wherever you buy books.